About the author

I was a Hampshire police officer for 30 years, retiring in 2011 as a Detective Chief Inspector. In the police, my particular interest was the control and management of sexual and violent offenders and the investigation and support for vulnerable victims, such as domestic and child abuse victims. I am fascinated by the inter-relation between Dangerousness and Vulnerability. After retiring from the police, I became a safeguarding trainer for children's services but was forced to stop working when I was diagnosed with Multiple System Atrophy; this condition has inspired me to write. I am married to Debbie, we have three daughters, a dog and two cats. We live near Winchester in Hampshire, UK.

CHAMELEON

Mark Ashthorpe

CHAMELEON

Vanguard Press

A CIP catalogue record for this title is
available from the British Library.

ISBN 978 1 784655 31 0

Vanguard Press is an imprint of
Pegasus Elliot MacKenzie Publishers Ltd.
www.pegasuspublishers.com

First Published in 2019

Vanguard Press
Sheraton House Castle Park
Cambridge England

Printed & Bound in Great Britain

For my wife and family without whom nothing would be possible.

Acknowledgements

My heartfelt thanks go to Helen and Tanya who shared the task of being the first people to read my book, and also to Margaret and Nicola for being the next batch of readers. I am eternally grateful for all of their insightful and invaluable feedback.

Chapter 1

Just three months ago Dave and Helen were sitting in his beige Morris Marina, in the dark corner of a remote Leeston Forest car park. They leaned towards each other to kiss passionately, Dave's right hand tentatively slid up Helen's short skirt, heading towards her knickers.

"I can't stay long, I said I was only nipping out to see Pam," Helen said. Pam was the usual excuse for their spontaneous and urgent rendezvous together. Pam was in on their secret and was considered reliable and trustworthy.

Dave's hand paused on her thigh. "Not even enough time for a quickie?"

"Well, I don't know about that," she giggled.

Taking this for assent he unbuttoned her blouse revealing her lacy, red and cream underwear. He knew this was part of a set of her best underwear, a sure sign that she was up for some fun.

They both wriggled over to the back seat and started to remove each other's clothes.

As they did so another car pulled into the car park, its lights briefly illuminating the couple. The car parked up on the other side of the car park but left its side lights on. "Bollocks!" Dave said, spooked by the new arrival, passion dramatically dwindling. "Let's get out of here," he said.

To them, it didn't seem possible that that time in the car park was only three months ago. At that time, they had both loved the excitement and thrill of sneaking around and snatching opportunities to be together. Now things had moved on, and they were in the much more serious and tricky business of dismantling their old lives and trying to make a new one together. Unfortunately, people were being hurt which was never their intention. But they had no excuse, they should have been able to predict the effect of their infidelity. The fact was, that they were so absorbed in each other, that no one else was in their thoughts, including their children.

Shaking, either through fear or cold, or maybe both, Mickey Williams lay on his bedroom floor with the curtains drawn, even though it was daylight outside. The bedroom was small, little more than a box room. There were books, toys and clothes scattered everywhere. Mickey had cleared enough space to lay down and stare up at the vague outlines of his posters on the walls. They were mainly football themed, specifically his team, Liverpool and a couple of his favourite players, Ray Clemence and Emlyn Hughes.

He was lying there waiting to be punished by the boy next door, who sat calmly on Mickey's small bed. The boy was twelve, only a couple of years older than him but seemed altogether more mature, knowledgeable and, above all, dangerous. He was called "the boy next door" because his mum wouldn't ever allow his real name to be said in her presence. The boy had told Mickey that he had to be punished because Mickey's dad was bad. He said that because Mickey's dad was no longer around, Mickey was to be punished in his place. Mickey had no idea why his dad was bad but thought that it must be the reason his dad had left them. His mum had cried and shouted a lot at the time when his dad disappeared. He remembered her screaming at him on one occasion, that it was all Mickey's fault, that his dad would have stayed if it wasn't for him.

His mum had told him firmly that the boy next door wasn't allowed to come around, never under any circumstances. She said that his family were "not their kind of people"; but he came to the house anyway. When she went out to go shopping or to a friend, he'd come to the back door and Mickey simply felt compelled to let him come into the house. In those days his mum went out more and more often. "I'm allowed to have a life as well, you know," she'd say. Not that Mickey would have dared to challenge her right to go out. Whenever she left to have a life, she told Mickey to stay inside and not to answer the door. He would have to make his own tea. Leaving a ten-year-old alone at home would seem unthinkable nowadays, but this was 1971, and the world was different then.

Mickey was afraid of the punishment, but more confusingly for him was that he also took a small nugget of pleasure in what was happening. For some inexplicable reason, whatever the other boy did, the physical contact, even though it was painful, was still some sort of comfort to him. It is an uncomfortable taboo, however, to contemplate that abuse victims might take some pleasure in their experience. For Mickey though, the pleasurable part of it only increased his feelings of guilt, to the extent that he blamed himself entirely for what the other boy did to him.

In reality, Mickey was forced to submit himself to whatever punishment was deemed necessary. The punishment mainly involved being slapped around the head, punched about the body, as well as being touched around his private areas. This went on until the other boy decided to stop. This generally didn't take too long, maybe ten minutes, sometimes longer. The boy seemed to like it the more Mickey cried but made a point of comforting Mickey to calm him down. The punishment, of course, had to be a great big secret otherwise Mickey would be dead. Really, he would be killed if he protested or, God forbid, told anyone else, he knew that as a fact, no doubt. In any case, he wanted to keep the secret for himself as well. He didn't really want to try to explain to his mother what he instinctively knew, that what they were doing was very wrong.

Chapter 2

It was almost two years ago that Simon Shaw, the head of IT development at Anglo Allied Pacific (AAP) was patiently standing in his boss, Meryl Logan's office. Meryl was an attractive, intelligent, middle-aged African-American woman who had very little in common with Shaw. She was smart and sharp and had a corporate law background. He was all about the IT and not so good with understanding business. Shaw was average looking but was well dressed in his grey Tom Ford suit with brown Gucci shoes. This was the look he had adopted at the insistence of his wife, Anne, when he was promoted. She told him that he needed to look the part, as well as being good at his job. Shaw had an air of self-confidence and had every right to. He had a good job in London and a nice home and happy family life in Southshire. He was a little too smug and arrogant to be likeable, but he didn't mind, he knew he was well valued in the company and life was good for him.

AAP is a medium sized company providing IT hardware and technical support solutions for companies in the UK and the Far East. Testament to their success was that AAP rented one of the more expensive upper floors of a spectacular, modern office block in central London, and paid their staff well. The decor was dominated by chrome and leather with an open plan and very minimalist feel. The views across London were stunning on a clear day. Today was a bright, glorious day and Shaw enjoyed the views, being able to see the river Thames and the London skyline, including at least a partial view of St Paul's Cathedral.

Although the space was designed to be open plan, Meryl had her own office and this was where Shaw stood, waiting to be invited to sit down. Shaw didn't think that he got on very well with Meryl. He told people it was because he wasn't a corporate suck up. The fact was that she didn't like him because he was arrogant and his passive/aggressive manner towards her gave her the strong feeling that he was a misogynist, who had little respect for her because she was a woman. Meryl was concentrating busily on her screen, ignoring Shaw's presence.

No invitation to sit was forthcoming so Shaw said, "So what's this all about, why do you want to see me?"

Meryl looked up and said frostily, "I don't, there are two gentlemen who want to see you, they'll be here soon."

Shaw was puzzled. "I wasn't aware of a morning meeting; did you check with my secretary? I'm not prepared."

"It's not a meeting as such, it's the police, they're the ones who need to talk to you."

"What, what about?" stammered Shaw.

"I'll let them tell you, shall I? I don't want to spoil the surprise." Meryl's face was now stony.

As if on cue, two men walked in. Shaw had a bizarre moment when all he could think was that they were both wearing cheap, ill-fitting suits. "Simon Shaw?"

"Yes, how can I help?"

They both held out their police warrant cards. "I'm DC McCartney," said one. "Simon Shaw, you are under arrest on suspicion of downloading indecent images of children." The other officer took hold of his arm and the first one started to read the caution. Shaw heard nothing much else after he was arrested though. He felt a wave of nausea and a roaring in his head, for this was the moment when his world fell apart.

Chapter 3

I still consider myself to be lucky, I know you won't believe it when you hear my whole story. I've had some ups and downs, but on balance I still think it's true. I think you should always count your blessings and I have had some very good fortune along the way. One thing is that recently I have inherited this great cottage from my mum, Helen. Thanks, Helen. Not that I have anything else to thank her for because she abandoned us when I was only eight years old. I hated her for this and despised my dad for letting it happen. But I think I can forgive her now because of my cottage. I'm like that, very magnanimous.

After Helen left us, me and my dad were alone together, I'm not sure who was more scared. Dad had never been the most hands-on of dads, he was what could be described as a traditional father. He was always uncomfortable around children and never really understood the complex, myriad needs of what it took to parent a child… me. He was a cold man, not cruel, just cold, incapable of showing affection. Before Helen left he saw his sole job in the family as the wage-earner, the breadwinner. This left Helen to do all the childcare, but that wasn't what she really wanted. She wanted excitement and fun, but these things were in scant supply where we lived and having to look after a child certainly didn't fit with her vision for her own life and future.

So, Helen ran off with the next-door neighbour, Dave Williams. He was unsurprisingly known locally as "Dirty Dave". Personally, I think it's disgusting what they did, and that going with Dave was frankly just a little bit lazy. I mean that if she really wanted to go off with someone she could have looked further than next door. Because of his job, Dave was around in the daytime, while my dad was at work. It seems to me that it was simply the convenience. It turned out that they had been having an affair for years. Funny word that "affair", it sounds so romantic and exciting, it doesn't sound like the sordid betrayal that it actually was. Their selfishness blighted the lives of our two families. Because of their actions dad and I suffered, but so did Dave's family, especially his son, I made sure of that.

Dave had a bit of money put aside so he and Helen moved away from the area and bought a rundown cottage somewhere in the country. I was told it was just along the coast near Leeston in the Leeston Forest, not really very far away in terms of distance, but a world away from us and far enough to be out of my life. Back then I had never even gone to the cottage, and dad would never speak of it. I only saw the place after Helen died and I found out that she had left it to me.

When I was growing up we lived in a two-bedroomed house in a grim, dull, council estate on the outskirts of Swinton. In case you don't know, Swinton is in the county of Southshire, it is the largest city in the county. Swinton is a sprawling coastal town with a large commercial dockyard and for this reason was bombed extensively in the Second World War. Growing up there I think I was oblivious to its history, I just knew that I hated it and I had to escape from that life as soon as I was able.

I also hated school and never made any real friends. I was obedient and compliant which meant the teachers liked me. I didn't like them much though. Growing up, I stayed out of the limelight and prided myself on being middle of the road at everything, staying under the radar – invisible.

The county of Southshire can be charming. Nestling quietly in the heart of the south coast of England; I love the countryside areas. Driving across the county you come across areas of outstanding natural beauty, with stunning rolling hills, and ancient verdant Forests, where once kings had hunted. The county epitomises all that is good about the English countryside, in my opinion.

We didn't live in the countryside, though, we lived in an area of outstanding natural ugliness. The council estate we lived in was a sprawl of social housing not designed for pleasing aesthetics, more for egalitarian, hard-wearing utility. It wasn't that the area was particularly dangerous when I was young, but neither was it particularly safe. The people were normal, on the whole. Drunks and criminals were in the minority but were vocal and more visible on Saturday nights. The residents were mostly the sort of people who went to work, had families and lived unremarkable lives. Sadly though, in recent years the drug dealers and the gangs have moved into the area. Living in parts of the estate now was like hell for many of the residents, particularly the elderly, some of whom live like prisoners, fearful in their own homes. That's progress, I suppose.

Growing up on the estate was what was normal to me, but even then, I had no plans to remain there. I saw myself somewhere, almost anywhere else, so I moved away as soon as I could. I also had no thoughts of being normal. I had plans to be my own person and do my own thing, to be someone exceptional. I didn't want to be like everyone else because I wasn't, I knew that I was different, but I also knew I had to hide that difference to survive.

Of course, I didn't know it at the time, but Helen was bored to death with Dad. I think it was this boredom that eventually forced her to leave. This should not have been surprising to me as my father was an exceedingly dull and boring man. He had no hobbies or interests outside of work apart from his garden, which to be fair, was very well kept and looked nice… if you like that sort of thing. Dad had worked in the same warehouse, for the same company for forty-five years until his retirement. He'd started work there as a young apprentice and with a high degree of diligence, but very little ambition or imagination, he worked his way up to the position of warehouse manager. Logistics, the storage and movements of goods and transport was his special talent, but it started and stopped there. The company gave him, and us, a good enough living, but as it turned out had drained him of his best years.

When Dad finally stopped working, what should have been his quiet, peaceful retirement gardening turned out to be anything but. Dad had always smoked and had a long-standing chest cough. When he finally saw a GP, there followed swiftly the most dreaded diagnosis. Dad had cancer which had gone undetected for a long time, so had spread far enough to be inoperable. Dad was clear that he didn't want to undergo chemotherapy as he said it was poison and didn't see the point of prolonging the agony. There was no persuading him otherwise, believe me I tried, but Dad lost most of his will when Helen left. So instead there was a short period of illness, then a quick and, maybe, merciful death. It seemed unfair to me that he had worked hard to reach retirement, then had it stolen away from him in such a brutal manner. He had plodded on in a dull, pointless job for all those years, and for what? An early death, and no payback for his hard work. That wasn't for me, I was now old enough to make my own decisions and wanted more than my dad ever did.

I left soon after he died to make my own way in life. In fact, the council sent me a letter asking me to vacate the house because they needed it for a family. At the time I thought that the letter was a bit cold-hearted, but I didn't care, I wanted out in any case. Dad left me some money but not enough to change my life. Helen's cottage will change my life, though.

Looking back now, I think that living with us Helen could see her future mapped out before her, (not about the cancer, of course) and her choice was clear, us or the neighbour, boredom or excitement, life or atrophy. But, I can forgive Helen now because of the cottage – does that make me shallow? Maybe, but it is perfect, exactly what I wanted, what I have fantasised about.

The cottage is near Leeston in the middle of the Forest about ten miles from where we lived in my childhood but, as I said, a world away from our estate. The cottage was quiet and out of the way, with no neighbours nearby. It had become even shabbier and overgrown with time, but it was perfect for me. You might not see what I see in it, though.

Peach Cottage is a rundown 1930s bungalow set in about an acre of overgrown, jungle-like garden, rambling and ramshackle with several crumbling outbuildings. One of the outbuildings contains a couple of rusty old cars, surrounded by piles of assorted junk, accumulated from God knows where. The cars were 1970s vintage British Leyland; a beige Morris Marina and a green Austin Allegro, they were the unfortunate offspring of what was, at the time an ailing British car industry. The cars were now decaying from old age, relics from an age gone by – that's what this place is all about, decay and death. This suits me, I like it, you might not.

As you negotiate the broken wooden double gates to the weed-embedded drive you see the paint peeling from the cottage walls. The place is large and double fronted and the nameplate "Peach Cottage" could just about be seen, being mostly obscured by foliage. A shade of peach is the colour you can see from the few patches of wall peeking out in between the ivy and wisteria which seem to be jointly devouring the house. Entering the hallway through the faded blue front door you stop in your tracks as you are hit by a solid wall of smells and sights. The atmosphere inside is thick and palpable, your senses are overwhelmed by the interior. I gagged the first time I walked in, the sickly-sweet smells assaulted my senses. You can almost physically feel the various states of putrefaction that exist in the place.

You see, Helen had become a hoarder. When they bought the cottage, it was in a poor state of repair, but it only went downhill from there. Dave was not keen on DIY or gardening, so none of the jobs around the house ever got done. What had drawn them together, the desire to make a perfect home together, eventually drove them apart. They were both feckless dreamers and, over time, the atmosphere between them became toxic. When Dave finally had enough, he moved on and left her in the cottage. At that point, time stopped for Helen. It literally stopped for Helen, this was in 1976. The long, hot summer that everyone has such fond memories of, that is everyone except Helen because that was the time when her dreams fell apart.

Everything that people usually do, was exactly what Helen was incapable of doing. Paying bills, decorating, cleaning, gardening, throwing rubbish away were all beyond Helen. Can you imagine what you can collect in forty years of living like a hermit? Gas and electricity had been turned off years ago, as no bills were ever paid, and were said to be unsafe anyway. She was all alone apart from an assortment of animals. She had a dozen or so cats, four old dogs of various breeds, and a goat. Helen had had a mental breakdown, the GP told me almost apologetically, whilst at the same time trying to justify their own negligence. When Dave left she just simply lost it; she lost her mind, her dignity and most of all her hopes for a better future.

The community nurse was meant to make regular visits to Helen because she'd developed several health problems, including mental illness. Eventually, it was she who found Helen's lifeless body in the bedroom, where she'd already been dead three weeks. That's what hoarding does, it stops people coming around, keeps you isolated, leaves you dead three weeks with no one to care.

Not that I had any contact with Helen after she left us. She never once tried to get in touch with me. No letters, phone calls, Christmas or birthday cards. Do I have unresolved issues about this, am I angry? I was angry, for sure, but less so now, not now that she left me the cottage. The solicitor said that the cottage was mine because of a will she'd written a few years ago. She simply left everything she had to me, does that mean that she really had cared for me? I suppose there was no one else, though, and that meant the cottage was now mine.

Of course, the first thing I had to do was to get rid of the animals. That was quite entertaining, I must admit, except I couldn't find all of the cats. I only ever found three of them, and they were the old ones, I have no idea where the rest went. They must have had some sort of sixth sense to know what was in store for them and made good their escape. This was also my first garden burial, well there anyway.

Thinking back on my life, I will tell you that I was bitter and angry when Helen left with Dave. Using my anger, I got some small revenge. Dave had left behind a young boy when he bailed out. Do you know what can happen to a child if their misbehaving dad leaves them unprotected? Well, they get punished, it's only fair. I couldn't get revenge on Dave, so I went for the next best thing. So, Mickey became the surrogate, and I found out something about myself into the bargain. I had found my vocation in life, my passion, something I loved to do, and it had nothing to do with gardening, believe me.

So, why do I think I am so lucky? It's not just that I now have this extraordinary, mortified, ruin of a cottage, but to my delight and amazement it has something I'd only ever dreamed of. I never imagined I'd actually ever have one myself. It's a bit of a fantasy of mine, you see, you might even say an obsession. It has a cellar, a cellar was something that suited my needs perfectly, something I have a great use for.

Walking through the front door with its ancient peeling paint, the smell hits you hard but this is all good for me. The smell helps keep people away. It seems that when they bought the cottage it was a mess and had never been updated since it was built. I walked through to the kitchen, it looked like a rotting museum of days gone by. The cottage's electrical system was ancient. Originally wired in 1930 it had Bakelite switches and sockets throughout, along with the original wiring looms. That is all very well, but my eyes quickly land on what I have been eagerly anticipating. In the corner of the kitchen there is a small wooden door, once painted white now faded to yellow, this door leads to the cellar. A short, tight staircase then takes you down to the musty depths of this wonderful place – my own wonderland – my palace. It's not big, but it doesn't need to be, only about four metres square, but you can stand up easily. The walls are whitewashed, and a bare light bulb relieves the gloom, but only slightly. It smelt strongly of dampness and stale air, much like a prison cell. In the far corner of the room is an old, stained mattress with a pile of rags on top.

A pair of large, round, brown eyes suddenly open in the rags and a small mewling sound commences. The pile of rags contains a seven-year-old girl who is small, thin and terrified. Her name is Ai, which means "a sentimental love". This, I think, is appropriate because I am a sentimental person and I have a lot of love in my heart, it just needs the right channels. Ai is understandably scared but there is no need for her to be … providing she doesn't cause me trouble. Of course, she doesn't cause me trouble, though. By the time Ai reached me she was no longer really a seven-year-old child, she had already lived and suffered several unhappy lifetimes, starting from the moment she was taken away from her home six months before.

I was told that she came from Sa Pa which is in the Lao Cai province in Vietnam. When I found out where she came from, I looked it up. Wikipedia tells me that Sa Pa is a popular tourist trekking base near the Phang Xi Pang peak, which is climbable via a steep walk. Sa Pa overlooks the stunningly beautiful terraced rice fields of the Muong Hoa Valley, but poverty is rife there, making the locals ripe for exploitation. Trafficking is a way of life for many, and Ai's fate is by no means exceptional. Her family loved and cared for her as well as they could, but they had very little themselves. They had basic shelter, little food and barely any money. Seeing an opportunity to have one less mouth to feed, and a better life for Ai into the bargain, seemed like the best thing to do. Ai had been sold by her parents for just a few dollars. The traffickers promised a happy life in the West where she'd live with a family and get an education. Did her parents really believe that, though?

The promise of a happy life has partly come true for Ai. She's happy with me now because I cherish and look after her. I would never want to harm her, I would never do anything she didn't want. Of course, I quite enjoy my time with her, and she enjoys our games because I am gentle and kind. I would never hurt a child, it's not in my nature, I love children. Children are so much easier to deal with than adults. Adults are too complex and confusing.

I have to tell you this, even though you'll think I'm a selfish hypocrite... but Ai is just not enough for me. I bought Ai on the open market – yes, it's easy to buy trafficked children if you know where to look, who to talk to. I know exactly where to search on the darknet to find the kind of people who took Ai. If you've never heard of the darknet, it's like the evil twin brother of the world wide web. It exists for illicit activities just like this, the darknet overlays the internet but leaves no internet footprint, so is safe for people like me to operate in, I can do anything, and I can't be traced. It's brilliant! With the right software you can share any images or buy just about anything you want; things that would be illegal in the real world, guns, drugs, children, whatever you want.

But I know what I want, I've known for a very long time now, I want to take someone for myself on my own, I want to abduct a child to keep captive for myself. You understand, if you're not doing it yourself where is the challenge, where is the hunt, the risk, the game? I need to make plans for the future but for now Ai will have to do for me.

Chapter 4

"Hi, I'm Alan," he said smiling pleasantly at the pretty woman as she sat down opposite him in the Busy Bean, the most popular café in the town, and which was about half full now.

She put out her hand to shake his. "Julie." She smiled a slightly nervous smile, which looked a little incongruous on her. Alan thought that with her attractive looks, she really should have more confidence. Maybe some bad experiences in the past had knocked her confidence, he wondered?

Alan was in his mid-forties, of average height and build, he had an open, honest face. He was clean-cut, slightly balding and smart, but casually dressed in chinos and brown jacket. He was very average looking and would probably pass unremarked wherever he went. He just looked like someone's dad, invisible to the rest of the world.

Julie, on the other hand, looked stunning. She was slim, late thirties, with long red hair and a figure-hugging cream knitted dress. Several men (and women) surreptitiously glanced her way as she took off her short, black leather jacket and hung it on the back of the chair.

The coffee shop was warm and snug with several comfortable brown leather sofas and armchairs. Most people occupied the sofas which were more intimate and relaxing, but this seemed a little too soon for Julie and Alan. So, by unspoken mutual consent, rather than that level of intimacy, they chose the safer option of a table and chairs in the middle of the room.

They had met each other through the local radio dating website. After signing up they entered their own information, then browsed the profiles of other aspiring dates. Having chosen each other they then started a dialogue. Alan, "honest and caring" was interested in Julie, "lively and vivacious". They then struck up an e-mail conversation to see if they were interested in each other or not. To Julie, "honest and caring" sounded better than the types of over-confident men she usually attracted. Even if one of those attributes were true that would be a significant improvement.

After her past failures and almost in desperation, Julie had decided to adopt a new tactic this time. Her latest plan, suggested by a friend, was to enter search criteria for the exact opposite characteristics of what she usually looked for in a man. Frankly, her usual searches only ever threw up hopeless, loser, bad boys – she had enough self-awareness to know that they were obviously her type, but she had to change because they were getting her nowhere. Instead of selecting "confident", "long hair" and "rock music" as descriptive preferences, she typed in "shy", "balding" and "classical music" instead – well she thought it was worth a try. What could possibly go wrong?

After some tentative e-mail ping-pong, they agreed on a safe first date in the Busy Bean in Leeston. The town was convenient for both of them, it is a popular tourist destination and is usually busy enough to be a safe, neutral venue. They had both had previous bad experiences with blind dates and were approaching this encounter cautiously. When she first saw Alan, she was pleasantly surprised that he was normal looking and seemed nice enough.

"So, how many times have you done this before?" Alan asked.

"A couple of times, not very much," she said non-committedly. In fact, she had done this a half a dozen times, all with fairly disastrous results. A couple of the dates seemed OK, but none of them were interested in her when she told them she had two young kids. No need to drop that bombshell too soon today, she thought.

The Busy Bean coffee shop was in the middle of Leeston High Street. Leeston is a small but very pretty, unspoilt market town on the edge of the Leeston Forest national park, set on the river Lees. Leeston has held a charter since the Middle Ages to hold a market in the town, and the mainly Tudor beamed buildings that line the two hundred metres long High Street stand testament to the town's long history. The shops are all independent and unique, some even a bit quirky. There are no pound shops here, and the shops are very much oriented towards the tourist trade.

As it happens, Alan and Julie seemed to be very comfortable together, they chatted amiably, and, to her surprise, Julie found that she was actually enjoying herself. Even though they had only just met she found herself thinking that she could be mildly attracted to him.

Alan was easy company and was clearly intelligent, with a gentle sense of humour – not like her usual men! Alan and Julie chatted about their pasts – he told her that he was divorced but had no children. She took a deep breath, then told him about her ex-husband. She also talked long and fondly about her two beautiful young children, Kelly-Ann and Sam. To her amazement he seemed quite OK with the idea of children, he was even interested enough to ask about the usual things like their schools, friendships and hobbies, just like normal people do. He made the right complimentary noises when she showed him pictures of her children. Usually at this point, with the other men she'd had dates with, there followed some poor excuse then a slick departure soon after, never to be seen again. Men are so rubbish, but Alan seemed different, well who knows?

She found herself unloading stuff she'd never told anyone, even her friends. She talked about her ex-husband, Ricky. He was a scaffolder and a body-builder and loved to show off his great body. He was very good looking, with long black hair, worn usually in a ponytail.

He hit her occasionally if she tried to defy him, but it was usually an open-hand slap leaving no lasting marks. But mostly it was his controlling behaviour she found hardest to live with. She couldn't do anything by herself, she couldn't wear anything, go anywhere, or do anything without his permission. He justified this by saying that he loved her and needed to protect her and the kids, this was just his way of showing it.

He had rules for everything that she needed to abide by. The problem with his rules, though, was that they were constantly changing, and she never really knew what his reaction would be to any given situation. As a result, she was always on edge and became a complete nervous wreck. She lost weight and her skin was terrible. She suffered from anxiety and depression and became a shadow of her usual self. Her family noticed this change and tried to help but she became cut off from them, this was partly at Ricky's insistence, but partly because of her shame at her own weakness.

Luckily for her, it ended with Ricky when he walked out on them. He had found a young, pretty girl from the office of the scaffolding company. He'd been seeing her for a while and Julie suspected that the new girlfriend might be pregnant. For his part, Ricky said it was Julie's own fault because she had let herself go, the bastard. Julie felt sorry for his new partner – but at least she was off the hook. Even though it was the right thing for her, she fell apart when he left, but with support from her friends and family she eventually managed to get it back together. Ricky never paid any maintenance but thankfully he didn't show any interest in the kids either. So, Julie got a job that she wanted to do, rented a nice house, got well again then tried to move on with her life.

As Julie was talking animatedly about her kids and her life story, she noticed a short, scruffy man in his forties making his way towards them.

"Hello, Simon, nice to see you," the scruffy man said loudly, in a not very friendly way.

Alan looked uncomfortable and looked away from the man towards Julie with a look of hopelessness on his face. For a moment Julie glanced quizzically at Alan then turned towards the rude man, "Do you mind, we're having a private conversation!"

The man ignored her and said, "Is that so, Simon? Is this a new friend, someone that you're keeping from us?"

Julie became furious with the man's attitude, not least because he had simply ignored her. She was also upset that this man she'd started to like may have lied about his name.

"Does she know about your past?" the man asked.

Alan shook his head miserably. Julie was scared now as the horrid man turned towards her.

Before she could think of what to say, the man went on. "I don't know what he has told you, but this is Simon Alan Shaw. He's a Registered Sex Offender, a paedophile." He showed her his ID card. "I'm with the police, Detective Sergeant Paul Smith."

Alan (or Simon) interrupted, "Look she's an adult, I am allowed a private life you know."

"Not if what you're doing poses a risk," said DS Smith flatly.

"What risk can I possibly pose? We're having coffee, that's all, what is the risk in that?"

"I've got two children," Julie whispered, barely audibly.

"Sorry, what was that?" said Smith, having heard perfectly well what was said.

Julie seemed to make up her mind then said clearly and coldly, "I've got two young children. Alan... er, he seemed to take a lot of interest in them." She got up suddenly, grabbing her things then stormed out of the coffee shop.

Shaw's face reddened but he said nothing.

"Nothing to say?" said Smith, sitting down opposite him on the now vacant chair.

Shaw looked like he would remain silent as his jaw clenched and unclenched. Then in a harsh whisper he said, "Look, you're not allowed to do that, I have rights. I'll sue you and your Force. You can't just wreck my life like this, it's not fair, I have served my sentence, I paid the price for my mistakes, why can't you leave me alone?"

DS Smith's face went hard, he gritted his teeth and said, "Because you're a paedophile and you pose a risk. I will do whatever it takes within the law to stop you abusing children! That includes monitoring who you have contact with, particularly if you're trying to gain access to kids to abuse. My guess is she's a single mother?"

"But I have never touched a child in my life, I just downloaded some wrong stuff once," blustered Shaw.

"We do know from research that most online offenders either are already, or go on to become, contact offenders," said DS Smith.

"But I'm not most offenders," protested Shaw quietly.

By now the whole coffee shop was staring at the two men as they realised that something interesting was going on.

Aware of the attention, DS Smith said, "Look, I'll come and visit you tomorrow at eleven and we can discuss this. You must remember we have a written agreement in place, and in any case, your probation licence says you must notify us of any new relationships."

"All right," muttered Shaw as he got up and walked out of the coffee shop, which, as he left, returned to normal.

Chapter 5

Simon Shaw was divorced, that much he had told Julie was true. He had been married to Alice for thirteen years – unlucky for some. They had a beautiful boy and had been very happy together, or at least had all the outward appearances of happiness. Their son, Harry, was now six years old, not that he had seen Harry's last two birthdays. That's what hurt Shaw most, not being allowed to see his son, his own flesh and blood. He remembered when he was born, in truth Shaw was travelling at the time and had missed the birth, but he still thought that it had been the most wonderful and remarkable thing in his life. Now he was being denied any real contact with his own progeny.

It was probably fair to say that Shaw hadn't been the best of parents, he'd been too absorbed in work and his own problems and didn't invest enough time in home. He'd even missed a couple of family holidays because of travelling for work. Given the chance he would love to make amends and change all that now, but he wasn't being given the chance – that chance had been stolen from him.

Shaw looked around at the tiny rented flat he now lived alone in. He'd been a self-made man, he hadn't come from a family with money. He'd earned every penny he had, and before prison he'd had everything. He had a family, an executive five-bedroomed house in a beautiful area, his dream job, a company car, holidays and a wide circle of friends. At least people he'd thought were friends – but were they really friends? Now he was not so sure. They disappeared soon enough when he was arrested, it seems no one wants to stay friends with a sex offender. All his past was gone now, his life had been erased, he was left with nothing, how is that fair?

Alice had moved on quickly enough when he was incarcerated, obscenely quickly he thought. She pushed for a quick divorce which he didn't contest, and she had since remarried and moved to Colorado, which is apparently somewhere in America. He knew full well where Colorado was, but resented the place for being so far away. At least Alice could have waited a decent interval before abandoning him in prison. But she couldn't wait, instead she'd married a cowboy called Clay. The distance now makes contact with his son virtually impossible, particularly as he was not even allowed to use his computer for social media. He was allowed to Skype once a week from an internet café but that was not really good enough and, in fact, hadn't yet happened. How do you keep a relationship going with anyone in that way, let alone a child? A child's youth is so fleeting, you blink, and you miss massive changes. How was he to maintain any meaningful bond with his son?

He'd been a complete fool, he knew that now. He had worked very hard for the company, probably too hard. He travelled a lot for long periods, particularly in the Far East. He got lonely sometimes, so he went on the internet. Surely that's got to have been better than having an affair or going with prostitutes as some of his ex-colleagues did?

His biggest mistake was searching for porn on the work laptop, that and those DVDs he bought in Thailand. He'd seen some pornographic DVDs in a street market and just bought them on the spur of the moment. In fact, he'd never even opened the cellophane wrapper and didn't really know what they contained, albeit the cover picture of girls in school uniform certainly would have given him a clue.

So, what were the key low points for Shaw since it all went wrong? Having to admit to his idiot boss that he had gone onto porn sites on a work laptop; getting arrested at work and being frog-marched out of the building in front of his colleagues; seeing his wife and son's looks of fear and confusion when the police took him home under arrest to search the house? The list of ignominies is endless, and it never stops, it just keeps going.

Shaw had eventually been told that the police had found more than 50,000 pornographic images on his computer and 100 of them were of children. They also found the Thailand DVDs at the back of the wardrobe. Even though he'd not opened the packages, the pictures on the front cover were of girls in school uniform, so apparently gave supporting evidence that he was a paedophile.

Stupidly, all this happened after his laptop went in for an upgrade in his own department. His own department, where was the loyalty? For some reason, and outside of his remit, the technician saw fit to go through the laptop's browsing history, including deleted data. From what he found, the technician then told Shaw's boss that he thought that there was child porn there. His company went straight to the police without even asking him about it, they didn't give him a chance to explain. It was at that point in his life that everything changed.

Then the lawyer came along. Julian, the lawyer, was very well dressed and very well spoken, he was very confident, but he turned out to be very wrong. "Say nothing to the police", he said, "then we'll plead not guilty and go to trial. They've got to prove it, everyone gets off these now."

Why did he listen to him? Looking back now it seems so stupid. Julian hadn't been in court when Shaw tried to explain that he didn't know about the child images. The judge was clearly very pissed-off during the trial, making great significance of the fact that he'd offered no explanation, when interviewed, for the existence of the images. Apparently, he'd been warned that he needed to give his explanation to the police, but how was he to know? He just followed the advice Julian gave him. The good news was that the judge seemed to cheer up when he sent Shaw to prison for two years. This sentencing was accompanied by a long lecture, of course. Alice came to visit him just once following his conviction, and that was only to ask for a divorce. Shaw found himself alone again while Alice quickly remarried and started a new life in America with her new husband and Shaw's son.

Prison was not really a barrel of laughs. Because Shaw was a "nonce" (prison parlance for a child sex offender), he was a "rule 43" prisoner. Prison rule 43 meant that he was a vulnerable prisoner, so he was segregated from his fellow inmates for his own safety. This was great in theory but was not actually easy to achieve. In reality prison was terrifying. Shaw could not sleep well, despite being exhausted, because of the fear. In films, the hero will make a friend who will support and protect them in the most troubling of times. Ha, no chance of that, in any case Shaw could not bring himself to be friendly with anyone he met. Aloof and suspicious, he actively avoided any overtures of friendship. How could he be friends with the types of people who were incarcerated in here, he thought? Shaw didn't get the irony.

In actual fact, he was only ever attacked once in prison. He was in a lunch queue when he accidentally stumbled into another prisoner. He'd been queuing for lunch with the rest of the inmates, minding his own business, when an argument broke out next to him. He was jostled into someone next to him – a middle-aged, small, thin man – accidentally knocking his tray of food onto the floor. With relief Shaw thought, thank God, it's not one of the huge thugs you see in here, he could have been in trouble. As it was, Shaw was over a foot taller than the little man. But he was wrong. The man came at him like a crazed dervish, punching, spitting and snarling. He punched Shaw repeatedly about the head and torso until he just curled up on the floor shouting for help. Shaw could hear cheering and shouting but no one came to his rescue, where were the guards? After what felt like an eternity the man stopped, held out his hand and said, "No hard feelings, mate? You knocked me dinner over."

Shaw was bleeding from multiple facial cuts but managed to stammer, "No, no hard feelings. Take my lunch."

The small man smiled like a child, "Thanks, mate." He then walked off as though nothing had happened. Shaw made his way to the infirmary following his accidental "trip and fall". He heard later that the man had once been a professional boxer, just his luck.

There were probably a lot of nonces in the prison, a lot more than were willing to admit to it. The attitude of the guards was somehow worse, though. As a prisoner he was beneath contempt, as a nonce he was below even that lowly status. The prison officers were not overtly violent, but they made it clear that violence could happen at any time. Shaw was constantly belittled and bullied, something that, as a proud man, he found difficult to take.

Shaw survived prison somehow, what doesn't kill you apparently makes you stronger. On leaving prison after a year on licence and with time off for good behaviour, Shaw didn't feel stronger, he felt degraded and empty. His life had exploded when he was arrested, in the balance book of life he had lost his wife, his child, his house and his job. On the plus side he had gained a probation officer, a police sex offender manager and lots of spare time.

In prison Shaw thought long and hard about what he would do with his time when he got out, it had to be something bigger and better than before.

Chapter 6

Detective Inspector Sue Taylor was in her mid-thirties, slim, attractive with blonde, short hair. Sue ran the Western Area Criminal Investigation Department which included the Public Protection Unit. This unit housed the teams dedicated to investigating child abuse and managing registered sex offenders. It was a demanding job but worth it, Sue had worked hard to get where she was but was ambitious and wanted to go further. She did not want Paul Smith to damage the excellent reputation of her and her team. She was very good at her job and was well regarded by her staff, but she was also aware that her many rivals would love to see her fail. Despite this, her philosophy was one of fiercely supporting her staff wherever possible. It was hard being a senior detective and harder still being a senior woman detective who was constantly judged, but rarely judged fairly.

Last year she'd had a terrible hiatus in her life when her charming, handsome surgeon husband had revealed his true nature. Following an argument, he had punched and kicked her, knocking her unconscious. The worst of it was that she hadn't seen it coming at all. He had just suddenly punched her in the face in the middle of one of their arguments. Once he had started, it seemed he couldn't stop himself. He punched her several times about the head then kicked her as she fell to the floor. She blanked out, which seemed to bring him to his senses. As she regained consciousness he was knelt over, hugging her and sobbing. He drove her to the hospital (not his own hospital, of course) where they described to the casualty doctor how she had slipped and fallen down the stairs.

In truth, she should have seen it coming as he was always prone to fits of jealous rage. This rage was usually directed at household objects, which she was used to just quietly replacing. No one suspected the truth of what had happened, and, to her shame, Sue found that she was unable to bring herself to report her husband. Sue knew well enough that part of the insidious nature of domestic abuse is that the victim is often not able to confront it, so abuse is rarely reported. In Sue's case, at least she had the strength to leave at that point, and never return. Partly because of her job, she was very conflicted about not feeling able to report her husband, but it gave her a real insight into the difficulties faced by domestic abuse victims. Victims less formidable than her, who were left powerless to protect themselves.

DS Paul Smith walked into her office, which was a drab, dull box. The only bright thing was a picture of Mount Kilimanjaro, which she had climbed the same year that she left her husband. This was hanging as a reminder to herself that she was strong and could overcome adversity.

"Paul, what on earth did you think you were doing?" Sue said in exasperation to the person she viewed as her best detective sergeant. She wore a smart, dark grey business suit and an air of genuine disappointment. Paul Smith was a talented detective and great offender manager, but he was a maverick. Yes, he dressed like a tramp, but he had a keen mind and a real passion for the work. DS Smith ran the team of detectives who managed the three hundred or so Registered Sex Offenders (RSOs), living across the patch. RSOs are people who have been convicted of a sexual offence and have to register with the police. The police then take on their management while they are in the community, using a number of tactics to prevent them from re-offending. Simon Shaw was one of those RSOs.

Paul looked down at his dirty, scuffed brown shoes like a naughty school child and offered, "But I was justified, I was right, I'm sure that he was grooming her to get to her kids!"

"Is that true, how do you know that?"

"Gut instinct."

"Is that all?"

"All? Ah, but instinct is the subconscious accumulation of observations without a conscious rationale. Instinct should never be ignored and can often be extremely valuable."

Sue shook her head, perplexed by her pontificating detective sergeant. "Don't lecture me, Paul. Gut instinct, however valuable, is not evidence, we work with evidence, we need proof. You were off duty and just blurted it out in public, you told everyone that Shaw is a convicted sex offender. You know you can't do that, there are procedures, authorities…"

"I used my initiative, I took a chance and went with it," he said firmly.

"You know as well as I do that we can't afford any vigilante activity, you know what's happened in the past."

"In Leeston, are you kidding, it's not Paulsgrove, you know?" Paul laughed, and Sue smiled faintly.

Early in the new millennium, Sue Taylor was working as a DS in Paulsgrove when there had been massive riots in the area. Paulsgrove is a housing estate to the east of the county near Portsmouth. The riots happened because a national newspaper "outed" a convicted sex offender who lived there. The newspaper had published his details as part of their "Sarah's law" campaign for the right for everyone to know where convicted sex offenders live. This campaign was started after the abduction and murder of Sarah Payne. On reading this information the local populace rose up in riot to get this man removed from the area. Ironically there were known convicted sex offenders involved in the rioting, blending in with the mob for safety. Following this event, the authorities were very cautious about revealing sex offender information in an unmanaged way.

They'd got over the crisis, she said what needed to be said, then added finally, "Seriously though, just get an authority next time, yes? Now get out," she said smiling, "I need to send an apology and cover your arse!"

Paul walked through to the main office where half a dozen detectives were pretending not to have been listening to their boss's exchange.

As he made himself a cup of tea he spotted an unfamiliar figure coming into the office. "Get out," he growled. "You're not allowed in here."

"But I'm your new detective, DC Webb, Nick Webb."

"In that case DC Webb, Nick Webb, you're very welcome... Tea?" said Paul, smiling, happy to have cleared the air with Sue.

Nick was in his early fifties, he was tanned and good looking and had a distinguished look which few men achieve. He was of medium build and height and looked as though he kept himself fit.

"Nick, I don't know what you've done to get yourself sent here but let me tell you all about what we do. I'm guessing it will be different to anything you've done before."

"I know that you take out paedophiles, and that's good. I hate paedophiles," Nick stated. "In fact, I volunteered for the posting, I needed a new challenge."

"Well you're partly right but we don't "take people out", we manage the risk that sexual offenders pose." Paul started to settle into his prepared lecture, something that he enjoyed doing. "There are about 50,000 registered sex offenders in the UK and about one-fifth of those are in prison. The rest live in the community and may or may not continue to pose a risk, that's the tricky bit, working out who poses a risk and who doesn't. We work with other agencies to manage risk and we make sure that sexual predators have no room left to offend in. We deny them opportunities to make more victims by being proactive, imaginative and lawfully audacious," he ended with a flourish.

"So, what does that really mean?" said Nick. This was way out of his comfort zone and area of experience, but he seemed keen to learn.

"If you assume that the sexual offenders will want to re-offend we have to reduce their opportunities and motivate them not to do so. In fact, the re-offending rates of sexual offenders are very low. That's because we spend all our time denying them opportunities to offend. Just yesterday I saw one of our RSOs with a new woman he hadn't told us about, so I told her about his past. Unsurprisingly, she had two young kids who undoubtedly, he was trying to gain access to. We have written agreements with our RSOs saying they must commit to being open and honest. For example, they must tell us about any new relationships, employment or hobbies, in fact they must tell us anything that impacts on their risk. The reality is not what you read in the news, in fact they look just like anyone else, you can't just spot a sex offender, they are not all dirty old men in raincoats. In fact, very few are. RSOs are like chameleons, they try to blend in well with their surroundings, so they can't be seen, but it's our job to spot them, then carefully watch them."

Surprised, Nick said, "I like the sound of that, but what about their human rights?"

"What about the victims' human rights? I know where my priorities are. Well, we'll soon get you properly trained, you can shadow some visits to get an idea of what it's all about, but you'll get a caseload straight away. In fact, the guy I was telling you about, Simon Shaw, will be on your caseload."

Paul showed Nick around the office, introducing him to the team. Nick met DC Helen Jackson, an experienced DC in the team. "You got any questions, ask Helen. If she can't help, ask me." Helen smiled at Nick who responded in kind.

Paul decided to avoid the DI, thinking he should let her calm down for a little bit longer. It was really good news to get a new staff member as workloads were high, and Nick seemed OK. Workloads were way too high, and it was a strain on everyone, sickness was higher than average but carrying such risk all the time can be too much for anyone, particularly when things go wrong, which sadly they do. Even if you know it's not your fault, you can't help but feel some responsibility. Paul knew what that felt like from bitter experience.

The Independent Police Complaints Commission had investigated Paul last year; that was a hard time, but the worst of it was knowing that he'd made a mistake, he'd got it wrong. Even when the IPCC eventually cleared him of any misconduct, Paul still felt guilty. One of the RSOs his team were managing seemed to be doing well, he was on licence from prison and the offender manager persuaded Paul to lower his risk level to low. This meant the RSO had significantly less contact and scrutiny from the authorities.

Beating himself up, Paul thought that he should have asked more questions at the time. His DC had told him that the RSO had a home, had a job, was drug-free and had a new girlfriend, who was in her thirties and was thought to be a good influence. She had no convictions, no kids herself and had been told all about his convictions which were all against children, so she was not assessed to be at risk. It all went wrong, it turned out that she was a part-time learning support assistant at Leeston primary school. The RSO had been going into the school with her and had managed to contrive to have significant contact alone with several vulnerable children. The head teacher had become suspicious of him when he kept turning up at school, and the truth came out when she contacted the local police to check on him. Thankfully, it was believed that none of the children had been harmed, but the head teacher complained to the Independent Police Complaints Commission saying the police were negligent. That's when he came to really respect DI Taylor, she stood by him when her bosses wanted to throw him to the wolves. They wanted an easy scapegoat, and it would have been him but for Sue Taylor. She stood by him and her trust was rewarded when he was cleared of wrongdoing.

Although Paul had been cleared, he still felt the weight of responsibility. He understood the fact that if dangerous people get released into the community then some will inevitably re-offend, and that's why managing sex offenders is so important to Paul, in fact it's his obsession.

Paul was married, past tense, very past and very tense. He was only married to Jane for a very short time, though. Married life didn't suit him at all, he just didn't really see the point. He only got married because Jane wanted to, and he felt obliged to agree. He was quite happy to just jog along with life, but that was just him. Jane thought differently, she had very different ideas for their future. Jane was a bank clerk and they'd met at a friend's party.

Both were shy but were introduced by their host and managed to strike up a conversation. They had both been drinking so were more relaxed with each other than otherwise would have been the case. This, Paul would often argue, was even more evidence of the social harm consequences of alcohol.

That night Paul had managed to summon the courage to ask Jane out, and so it started. They meandered their way slowly into a relationship and they'd got on all right. Jane was quiet and fairly serious, which suited Paul, who was not very outgoing. They became close friends, so after a while they drifted their way into marriage. Jane turned out to be not so quiet, in fact, he found she had rather a lot to say, particularly about his shortcomings. She tried her best to smarten up his appearance, but she was met with stiff resistance. After a very tricky two-year period it ended when Jane walked out on him. She complained that he was indifferent towards her and didn't really love her. She was right, of course. When she left him, Paul happily resumed his solitary life, worrying about no one but himself... and his RSOs, of course. The risks he juggled made his job interesting and challenging.

Chapter 7

Shaw was sitting quietly in Browsers internet café at just before four p.m. waiting impatiently for the agreed contact time with his son, Harry. Browsers was in Swinton in a trendy area near the university. It seemed less like a café and looked more like a workplace, with about a dozen workstations neatly arranged and separated by screens. There were three earnest looking young people there working, wearing headphones for privacy. As part of his prison licence conditions, Shaw was not allowed to access social media but had permission to use an internet café for contact with his son.

He had agreed with his ex-wife the time for a Skype call, which would be nine a.m. in Colorado. This was so that he could find an open café and it not be too early in America. He was worried that there was only a short window of time, but it could work, and he had to give it a chance. It all seemed quite reasonable, but this was their first attempt at this and he wasn't one to trust others very much, especially his ex-wife.

Shaw took a deep breath then dialled the number, dead on four p.m. There was no reply, but patiently Shaw tried again a minute later, there was still no reply. At around 4.40 Alice finally answered, she was looking annoyed, but Shaw by now was seething with anger. Alice, seeming to pre-empt an outburst said, "Don't start, Simon it's been a hell of a morning, we only just got back."

"But you knew I was calling at nine, how could you do this, the café closes soon?"

"Well, we could argue about that, or you could talk to Harry?"

"Put him on then."

Harry seemed to be dragged reluctantly to the webcam, presumably by Clay. "But I don't wanna." Shaw heard, and his heart froze.

As soon as Shaw saw his son, he quickly said, "Hi, Harry, it's Daddy."

Harry appeared to be confused and looked to his left where Clay must be stood. "Daddy?"

Alice interjected to explain in a condescending tone, as if to a child, "Simon, you're confusing Harry, you must understand that Clay is now Daddy, we call you "Simon". For accuracy, we refer to you as the birth father."

Shaw was bright red with embarrassment, frustration and anger but managed to hold it together enough to speak. "Harry it's Simon, your father. I want to tell you how much I love you and miss you."

Harry said nothing, so Shaw just rattled on asking questions and talking patiently trying to make a connection. Shaw hadn't prepared anything but focused on things he thought would occupy his son's time and thoughts, school, friends, hobbies. It was a Herculean effort but Shaw stuck with it right up to the point that the waiter walked up to him. He was a long-haired teenager wearing a red T-shirt, emblazoned with the words "Jamie" and "Cybarista" across his chest. He sidled up to Shaw nervously and said, "Sorry, mate, we're closing." Shaw became aware that he was the only customer left in the café and that they'd already cleared up.

Alice had obviously overheard this as she quickly interrupted, "OK, in that case, goodbye, Simon." And the connection was abruptly closed. That was it, nothing more.

Shaw sat there for a moment feeling a bit stunned and emotional. He was aware of the barista loitering nearby waiting for him to go. "My son… in America," stuttered Shaw in explanation. There was no reply and Shaw left quietly, the door was locked quickly behind him as he left.

Chapter 8

I sat in the kitchen with the peeling blue, pink and red-flowered wallpaper, eating a limp cheese sandwich and drinking a cup of tea. I thought about things, life, my past, my future. I'd had real ups and downs, but for the first time in a long time I had a plan, my mind was made up and I had a clear idea of what I wanted to do. I read the newspaper for want of anything else to do, it contained the usual mix of nonsense and sensationalism and nothing of any real interest to me.

As I opened the door to the cellar the smell was overwhelming, but with no ventilation this was inevitable. In the gloom I can see Ai slumped in the corner. She does not seem afraid now, just empty and resigned to her fate. Her eyes were devoid of either intelligence or emotion as she waited for whatever was in store for her, shivering slightly. I felt no pity for her because I had improved her life in so many ways – she came from the gutter and was abused by everyone she ever met. Her own mother sold her, at least I gave her some shelter, warmth and yes, love.

I turned the light on, then climbed down the stairs. Ai did not move at all but did not take her eyes off me. I grabbed her stick-thin arm – she must only weigh about four stone – and pulled her up to me. She opened her mouth as if by reflex, but not today. I'd had enough of Ai, she was only ever to be a temporary measure anyway, but I still felt disappointed, a bit cheated. The problem for me was that there had been no real challenge, she wasn't mine by right if I had to pay for her. I now had other ideas, something that would be truly satisfying, of my own making.

In fact, getting rid of Ai turned out to be surprisingly easy, I suppose being so small and frail I should have guessed but it was just as easy as strangling a small bird. It's funny but true. On the other hand, cats are tricky to kill, you have to watch the claws, and they fight like crazy. As for dogs, believe me, you don't want to even try to strangle a dog – they are tough buggers, even the smaller ones. One dog, a Yorkie called Fluffy, a neighbour's dog, bit me. Still, I got my own back on Fluffy – I cried hard and showed the bite off to everyone, complaining that he had viciously attacked me for no reason. Of course, Fluffy had to be put down as a dangerous dog, but you can't have dogs biting people, can you? Even if I was trying to break his neck. Not that I mentioned that bit, of course. I'm not going to lie, children are so much easier to kill than dogs.

The strangest thing is that Ai made no sound at all, she didn't put up any resistance even when it must have been obvious what was going to happen. She just looked at me with blank eyes. I'll never forget how she looked, no fear, just acceptance. How sad is it for Ai that she had simply resigned herself to death? She must have seen that all she had to look forward to, was just not to be alive any more.

How to dispose of the body, now that's a conundrum. Well thanks again, Helen, I smile at the thought. Of course, the garden, and it's good for the roses as well. I dug a shallow grave at the back, in what was once a flower bed near the kitchen window. As I buried her I am thinking that I should say a few words for Ai – how about?

Ai, she lived a little, not much, then died. There was a burial, but no one cried?

I laughed for a moment at my wit. Was this just a bit inappropriate really, not solemn enough for the occasion? As it happens I said no words. It is actually very tiring digging a deep enough hole, even when the soil is good. And here is a tip about body disposal – do not use quicklime, as you may have heard – it does not help get rid of the body, it speeds up decomposition, but can draw attention to it. So, I just wrapped her in an old sheet and buried her. It's amazing what you find out on the internet! Not that I am really a killer. Killing her was just the final chapter for Ai, it was easy but not a lot of fun, I'm not some weirdo who gets off on killing kids. I love kids, I wouldn't hurt a child for the world, except if I have to.

Digging the grave gave me a real thirst, it was a genuinely hard job, but worth it. She is now neatly put to rest, and I even planted a rose on the spot to mark her passing, as well as to disguise the digging, of course.

I went indoors to get a cup of tea. I sat in the kitchen again at the old Formica dining table with its matching chairs and thought about the future. What to do? I knew what I wanted, I always knew what I wanted, but do I dare? Would I, could I get away with it? I really did not want to get caught, that would not work out well for me at all. I had to be careful, but I can do that, I've been careful all my life. But do I dare? Of course, I dare, this is what I was born for, this is my whole raison d'être, as they say.

But who shall I choose, who shall be my target, my desire? Ideally, it will be somebody who deserves my love and attention. Not like dear Ai, she was just convenient, a useful commodity, I couldn't really love her – even though I gave her my love, I couldn't really love her. You don't always get what you want, though, and beggars can't be choosers sometimes. I wanted to be a chooser this time, though, not just take mail order potluck like with Ai.

I have been thinking about this for a very long time, I have some ideas about the future. You should understand that the children of single mothers make good targets. I have nothing against single mothers. It's not because they're negligent or bad parents but they can't possibly be everywhere at once. I have a lot of sympathy for single mothers. You can't blame them, but they need to have eyes everywhere. Single mothers need to get it right all the time, I just need to get lucky once, and you make your own luck, I firmly believe that. It just so happens I know of a single mum with two young children, either of whom would be fine for me. In fact, more than fine, it would be a dream come true.

Chapter 9

"So, Simon," said DS Smith, "this is your new offender manager, DC Nick Webb. He's going to be looking after you."

"That's very kind, but there's really no need, you know," Shaw responded casually.

They were all in the lounge of Shaw's small rented flat. It was just a few miles from his old house, but it might as well have been a thousand miles, or a lifestyle away. No one visited him, not one of his friends had made any contact with him at all, not even to wish him well. They used to know lots of people, but you never know who your real friends are until you're in trouble. Friends, they were obviously not, it seems that they didn't want to be tainted by any association with him.

He and his ex-wife had sold the house, so he had some capital, but he still needed to get a job, not least for his own sanity... and he needed to build a new life for himself.

DS Smith continued, "So what's this nonsense about you starting a new relationship without telling us?"

Shaw reddened. "I don't have to tell you everyone I see, I am a free man you know, I served my time."

Smith smiled. "Said just like an 'old lag', Simon. Listen, as we agreed when we first met, you have to be open and honest with us or we get worried about the level of risk you pose. And if I get worried I just need to go to court and apply to get a Sexual Offences Prevention Order to restrict what you can do, who you can see, where you can go. You don't want that, do you?"

A SOPO is a civil preventative order against convicted sexual offenders which allows the police to apply for conditions to restrict any activity that may lead to harm against children.

"But she was an adult!" said Shaw.

"She is a single mum with two young children... come on, who are you trying to kid? She said you were showing an interest in them."

"I was being polite," said Shaw blankly.

"Really?" interjected DC Webb with an unpleasant smirk on his face.

"Really!" repeated Shaw, glaring at Nick Webb.

"OK," said DS Smith. "Let's get on with the rest of the visit, then."

Shaw then showed the two detectives around the small flat. It had one bedroom, a bathroom, and a small lounge with a kitchenette in the corner. It was built about ten years before and was quite decent, it was reasonably decorated in magnolia for renting, but Shaw felt like it was a huge drop in standards for him to have to live there after where he used to live.

The detectives were looking for clues, any signs of children going to the flat or any evidence of Shaw showing an interest in children or using social media. In the bathroom they found two toothbrushes, which could be suspicious. When they asked him why he had two toothbrushes, Shaw explained that one was for scrubbing tight places in the shower. It rang true, Shaw was somewhat fastidious and to be fair, the brush head was black enough for this to be the case.

They got Shaw to switch on his laptop, then they put in specialist software to check if there were any child abuse images or any concerning search criteria like "young" or "child" on the laptop. The software would find anything suspicious even if it had been deleted. In fact, they found that Shaw's activity focused around two things: dating websites and job searches. The dating might be a concern, but Paul Smith filed that information away for later since they already knew about this. Paul opened a job-seeking website Shaw had been searching on.

"How's the job hunting?" said Paul, in a friendlier tone.

"It's not easy to get an IT job with a child pornography conviction," Shaw said.

Paul Smith bridled at Shaw's words, for he had inadvertently touched on a pet subject of his. "It's not pornography, the victims are not adults who can make choices. They are images of children who are being abused, and you encourage and support that abuse every time you download them. If you didn't take the picture yourself, you made it happen, you should remember that!"

Shaw wisely decided to say nothing to this. He hadn't been in prison long enough to get on the sex offender treatment programme, so was not as good at saying the right thing as those who had completed the course. He knew people who had completed the programme who could really talk the language and easily fool professionals. The question is whether they had really changed their behaviours, or had they learnt to better disguise themselves?

Smith continued to search the flat but found nothing of concern. Should the detective be happy with finding nothing? Then he spotted something of interest, a travel brochure for a cruise company.

"Caribbean cruises; are you going on a cruise?"

"Thinking about it."

DS Smith picked up the brochure and flicked through it. None of the cruises were advertised as adult only.

"Come on, Shaw, you must be joking? Why don't you just run into the street and shout, 'I'm a paedophile, somebody stop me'?"

Shaw looked bemused. "What are you talking about?"

"A cruise, are you kidding? What is a cruise ship but a floating hotel full of relaxed families, providing endless opportunities for you to exploit their kids? But seriously, this is honestly not a good idea for you. At the least, we'd have to notify the cruise company of your conviction so that they can keep an eye on you."

Shaw was angry now. "Is there no aspect of my life you won't try to screw up?"

"No there isn't, not if it stops you abusing kids," said Paul, bluntly.

As they were driving back to the office in Paul Smith's battered old Mazda, he continued with his lecture to DC Webb. "You see, it is all about control, we need to keep control of them. It is our job to put as many barriers as we can in the way of the RSOs. We have to make it difficult, if not impossible for them to re-offend. They will use all their energy and imagination to create opportunities to offend, we must spend at least as much time and energy to deny them these opportunities."

"By being lawfully audacious?" grinned Nick Webb.

"Oh, yes," said Paul. "Definitely!"

Chapter 10

Now that I have a purpose in my life, the game is on. I have made my mind up, and now is the time to start. I bought an old, white, Renault minivan and registered it in a false name and address. The van was small and unmarked. It was previously a decorator's van and is perfect for my purposes. I am always careful to park it away from home and certainly not near the cottage. I continue to drive my usual car for everyday use, the Renault is just for my "project" and I must use it sparingly. After all, I wouldn't want to be stopped in it, bearing in mind my plans.

I am careful where and how I drive, including avoiding motorways where there is likely to be ANPR – Automated Number Plate Recognition – I may be going a bit over the top but it's better to be safe than sorry.

I get to know the target area, both by car and on foot. I map it out to include footpaths and alleyways and plot the house as best I can, being careful to avoid lines of sight from their house and the neighbours' houses. After all, it wouldn't do to be seen.

They live in a small modern estate with a recreation park just over the road from their house. They are 1980s houses packed in claustrophobically together with postage stamp sized gardens. It's a quiet cul-de-sac, so very little traffic comes up the road and there are speed humps all along it. I never drive up the cul-de-sac. The park can be seen from the house but there is a blind spot towards the far end of the park where there is a cut through to the road beyond, that's where I will park. It's a few hundred yards away, but perfect for me to be able to get in and out without being seen.

As with any plan, it's Sod's Law that something, if it can go wrong, will always go wrong. There was just one minor cock-up yesterday. I filled the van up in the local garage hoping I wouldn't have to fill it again. My plan was to do my job then dispose of the van. But would you believe it, when I went to pay, I realised that I'd left my wallet at home? I convinced the cashier not to call the police, but to let me drive home then return immediately with the cash. Although it scared the life out of me, there was no harm done as I was only gone half an hour, and the garage attendant was OK about it. Even so, it was a mistake and one I didn't want to make, I didn't want to call attention to myself, but these things happen, and I got away with it.

Whenever I go to the estate I make a point of changing my appearance, nothing much, just different coats and sometimes hats. The trick with disguise is that you really don't have to overdo it – trust me – people just do not notice anything that doesn't directly affect them. My best disguise, though, is a dog. I signed up (in a false name) to walk rescue dogs from the local dog rescue centre. It's great, I don't like dogs, but I can come anytime to choose a dog to walk, and there are plenty to choose from. The dogs are pitifully happy to even get a small amount of time out, and the staff are friendly and grateful for the support. The thing is that it makes you invisible, people will recognise your dog but won't pay any attention to you at all. Also, you can go where you want or hang around as long as you like, and no one will challenge you.

Spending time in the estate I get a feel of the ebb and flow of the place. I get to recognise the comings and goings of families living there, in particular the stay-at-home mums and dads. My target works part-time and looks run ragged. The kids are often farmed out to child-minders and other local parents, but she still can't keep up. Genuinely, who could? It's an impossible task; thank God for that. What this means for me is that there are gaps in care – gaps I can exploit, if I'm clever and lucky – and I am clever, and as I said, I think I am lucky.

The kids are gorgeous, their mum is very attractive, and they have inherited their mum's good looks. To be fair I've never seen the father as he's not around – he may well be good looking as well. But they are perfect – as children should be. This is exactly what I need, beautiful, innocent, unspoilt. She is a bit older than her brother, she is eight and he is six years old, but they are slim and attractive – "Elfin" is the word that springs to mind. They look more like twins, they are the same height and build, and the age difference isn't obvious. She clearly has a caring role for her brother, as I see her often dropping him off with neighbours. He is obviously very attached to his sister, which I need to be wary of in case he causes a scene. It would be safer to deal with them separately, I think it's better to make sure that they are on their own, that complicates things a bit, but no one ever said this would be easy.

From my patient surveillance, I could see that when the weather was good she often took her brother to the park. I need them separated but there may be other kids around, the trick is to be invisible – I can do invisible, it's my forte, you'd say!

Chapter 11

"So, how's it going, Paul?"

DS Paul Smith was sat in the office of DI Sue Taylor and he was a bit nervous as the last time he was here was for a bollocking for revealing confidential information.

"All right," replied Paul, non-committedly.

"How's the new guy doing?" asked Sue.

"Nick?" Paul queried.

"Yes," said Sue "is he fitting in OK?"

Paul hesitated then said, "Yes, he seems very committed, very interested in the work. It's early days, of course, but he's showing a lot of promise."

"And what do you know about him, why did he transfer here?"

"He said that he wanted a new challenge," Paul said.

"Right, make sure that he's mentored and gets on the next offender management course, OK?"

"No problem." Paul wasn't at all offended by being checked on, in fact he admired Sue's thoroughness and her grasp of his work, something he considered to be his expertise.

Paul liked Sue and they'd often chat amiably. He knew that she had had a terrible ex-husband. Paul had heard that he was abusive to her, but she never told him herself, in fact she never talked about her marriage at all. It was before Paul knew her that they had split up. Paul had heard that he was a surgeon and was well respected, but you never can tell what people are really like and you never know what goes on behind closed doors. There had been rumours around the Force that he had put her in hospital after he had pushed her down the stairs. Although Paul hadn't known Sue then, he remembered it as a cause célèbre at the time, but gossip can also be very inaccurate.

He thought about his newest detective. Paul made a mental note to get to know Nick a bit better and ease his transition into the department.

Chapter 12

"Congratulations, I am pleased to say that you've got the job." A smiling Jon Davies stood up, leant over the desk and extended his hand towards Simon Shaw who was sitting, perplexed, on the other side. Jon was the managing director and co-owner, along with his brother, of Davies Engineering Industries. Shaw had just finished an interview with Jon but thought he had little hope of getting the job. Shaw had only gone to the interview because he had to as part of his prison licence conditions but was used to getting knocked back for one excuse or another. His CV was excellent, but no one wanted him with his conviction.

"You have got to be kidding me... why?" stammered Shaw.

"Sorry?"

"I mean why have you given me the job, you've read about my past right? Why would you trust me?" blurted Shaw.

Jon turned serious and said, "Because I was given a second chance once. I believe in second chances and I think that you deserve one. You're very well qualified and I think you can contribute to our success. This is an admin job, not what you're used to either in responsibility or salary, but it will be varied, and you'll be responsible for keeping our IT going. We're a small but growing company and it will be a challenge for you... if you're up for it?"

Shaw thought for a short while. This would be a huge step-down from his last job, the company was a modest manufacturing company based in a small industrial park near Leeston, but it was family-owned and seemed very friendly.

He broke into a grin. "I'd love to, it's amazing, sorry but I have been turned down so often because of my past, I can't quite believe it."

"And of course, we will monitor your internet activity in case you're tempted."

"No way, I've learnt my lesson, I won't let you down," Shaw declared solemnly.

"Besides I've spoken to Paul Smith..."

"What?"

"I've spoken to DS Smith and we're agreed that you're worth a chance." Seeing the look on Shaw's face, he continued. "Of course, we had to speak to the police and your probation officer, we've employed ex-offenders before, and they haven't all worked out well," Jon explained.

Shaw was torn now between joy at finally getting a job and annoyance that the police were still interfering in his life. Why can't they just let him alone?

"We'll need to run employment checks but when are you free to start?" asked Jon.

"I've got a couple of things to clear up but definitely next week?"

"OK, we'll keep in touch, we'll write with a formal offer, but I'm very much looking forward to working with you."

They shook hands again and Shaw thought about how busy he'd be before starting work.

Chapter 13

It was an overcast day but still quite mild. It was still school holidays towards the end of summer but not yet autumn. The estate was quiet as always as it was mid-morning and people were either at work or getting a daily fix of Jeremy Kyle or some similar form of daytime TV. I parked in the usual road in my usual spot, blending in as well as I could. I have no dog today so have a different disguise. Wearing a suit and tie and long coat, I'd hope to be seen as a salesman or similar.

Walking into the park, my stomach churns as I see children in the play area. My excitement is unparalleled, I am hyper-aware, my senses are so acute that I feel overwhelmed by the information I am seeing and hearing. I also want to enjoy the moment because I have dreamed of this for so long. I feel completely conscious of my body; my legs feel stiff and I struggle to appear normal. I'm fifty metres away and I try to walk unhurriedly across the field towards the play park. It's not easy, particularly when I catch sight of the boy, he's playing on his own, his sister is nowhere in sight. So, it's the boy, I thought, that's fate, it could just as well have been his sister. I'm secular in that way, I don't have an absolute preference. Having the boy will be wonderful, my mind fills with fantasies, soon to be translated into reality.

Thirty metres away, I can't help myself, I find myself walking faster. No one can see me, I am invisible, invincible, I am a predator and I am now stalking my prey. Twenty metres away I stop dead in my tracks as I hear a shout and a young girl comes running. Damn, it's the sister, this is terrible luck as it's too risky to try to take both at once. I veer away like a jet fighter and self-consciously walk back across the park to my van. All the way I expect to feel a hand on my shoulder, but none came.

I climb into the van, I am shaking and sweating, this was so close. I breathe slowly and eventually calm down. When I have stopped shaking I slowly drive off, but there is always another day.

The next opportunity I get is a few days later. I park the van in the usual road, look around then slip out quickly striding towards the park.

I took up a position in the cut-way, obscured from view but with a good line of sight to the play park. In the distance, I could see a couple of children in the park, but they were not my targets. It was a weekday, but the schools were still off, and the kids were keen to enjoy the last of their summer freedom.

I stood there for about ten minutes thinking that I'll need to move soon to avoid suspicion. My heart leapt, and my mouth went dry when I suddenly saw them cross the road to the park. I'm sure it's them, could there be any doubt? I had to calm down, I mustn't get too excited. I look around but I'm sure I can't be seen, and I know from my previous visits that this path is pretty much unused. As I am thinking this, an elderly man with a small dog came shuffling along the path towards me – would you believe it? I try to make it seem like I'm waiting for someone whilst at the same time keeping my face away from him and pretending to be on the phone. He mumbled "morning" as he passed me, and it was all I could do to stop myself from losing control of my bowels. I was shaking and sweating – I had to calm down, bloody hell, just my luck. I was annoyed at being seen but I made sure that he didn't get a good look at my face.

I took up my former position and could see that my children were still in the park. A few minutes went by, then it looked like the boy was saying something to his sister. The boy then ran off in the direction of a neighbour's house, it was a house I'd seen him go to before, and I guess the owner was watching the children for their mum. Hopefully not very well, though.

I was shaking and took a deep breath as I started to walk towards the play park. I walked steadily to the gate in the fence surrounding the play equipment and walked in straight up to the girl.

I was composed and calm as I said, "Kelly-Ann?"

She hadn't seen me approach and turned around suddenly, surprise on her face to hear her name. She looked at me but said nothing, sensibly not happy to talk to a stranger.

"Kelly-Ann, I'm David, a work colleague of your mum, Julie. She's had an accident and has had to go to hospital by ambulance. She asked me to come and get you and bring you to see her there."

"What's happened to my mum?"

"She fell and has banged her head, come on we need to go now."

She hesitated then said, "What about my brother?"

"He's at your neighbour's house, we already spoke to them to look after Sam, but you need to come now, your mother's in a very bad way."

She glanced around then made up her mind, if her mum's hurt she's got to go and see her! Besides, this man seems nice and seems to know her family and her mother well.

We walked briskly across the park towards the cut-way. Thankfully, the old man with the dog had disappeared and the other children in the play park paid us very little attention, so wrapped up were they in their own games.

Reaching the cut-way Kelly-Ann seemed to hesitate, so I smiled and said, "Come on let's go see your mum."

"Will she be OK?" she asked.

"Let's hope so, come on now, we need to get there as soon as we can."

We got through the cut-way and, thankfully, there was no one in the road beyond. Walking towards the van I feel in my pocket for the syringe. Once again, thanks to the darknet for this.

As we get nearer I waited until we were obscured by a high conifer hedge and the side of the van. I quickly pulled the syringe out of my pocket and injected her in the upper arm. Never having tried this before it was surprisingly easy, by luck she was only wearing a thin top.

I had practiced at home on oranges and that was actually harder.

She looked startled as I put the needle in but quickly seemed to go dizzy and disoriented. I opened the rear doors and spoke to her reassuringly. She seemed to fade out quickly and made no effort to call out or run. Her legs went to jelly and I eased her into the back of the van. I'd piled up blankets in the back and I covered her over so that she couldn't be seen if anyone looked in. I glanced around quickly to see if anyone was around. In doing so I realised that I was sweating badly as the sweat dripped, annoyingly into my eyes. I wiped it away with my sleeves and tried to calm down. Despite, or maybe because of the fear I felt, this was the most incredible rush I had ever had in my life. This was amazing, way better than I could have ever imagined. I had taken my very own, beautiful Kelly-Ann! She was truly my own, I had done all the hard work and now I deserve this fulfilment!

I pulled out of the estate slowly, being careful not to be conspicuous. I drove within the speed limits and took back roads to the cottage. It took a while and the drive was terrifying, but also exhilarating – now my new adventure really can begin!

Chapter 14

DI Taylor sat in her office with a deep frown on her face as the young officer briefed her on the Misper (Missing Person) report she'd just taken.

"Ma'am, Kelly-Ann Miles is eight years old, she went missing from a play park near to where she lives with mum and brother at about ten thirty this morning. She was initially reported missing by a neighbour who was watching the two kids while the mum was at work."

"It's a bit early to report her missing, why are you telling me now?" asked Sue Taylor.

"Ma'am, the sergeant said to tell you, it's because she was seen walking away from the park with a man. Her brother was with the neighbour at the time."

Hearing this Sue's interest increased. "Do we know who the man is?"

"No," said the officer. "Mum is single, and the neighbour doesn't know of any men connected to the family who would just walk off with Kelly-Ann. We spoke to mum on the phone and she doesn't know anyone either."

"Ex-partner or something?" said Sue.

"I don't know, someone's gone to mum's place of work to see her."

"Get mum home, we'll have lots of questions to ask her, and we'll need to search the house for clues. What are your thoughts on this?"

"I think it's a genuine abduction ma'am."

"In that case, we'll go with it, thank you for bringing this to me so promptly."

The officer looked pleased, but Sue was being serious. There is a principle in investigation that the "Golden Hour", the time just following the crime, is crucial in either recovering or losing evidence. This is especially important when dealing with missing children cases. Actions taken or not taken in those early stages are the difference between life and death. The fact is that children are rarely taken by strangers, but it does happen, and the police response must be swift. All these thoughts were rushing through Sue's head.

Sue stood up, walked to the door and shouted across the room, "Paul, get everyone back to the office now, it looks like we've got a child abduction."

Paul's eyes lit up. One of the perverse things about policing is that even when appalling things happen, the feeling of excitement at the thrill of the investigation can't be denied. Paul's mind raced with a hundred questions, but he knew he had to be patient. All will be revealed, and Sue was an excellent detective, so he had faith that they would get to the bottom of this latest mystery. He looked at the duty sheets to see who he had free. A couple of his team were working later, he'd call them in early, if needed.

A major incident room was established within Leeston police station, being the largest, most local police station. The station is a tired, sad, purpose-built building; constructed in the 1970s it is a brick and concrete carbuncle which could only be improved by demolition. Selling the station was always being considered because the location for redevelopment was excellent. As financial cuts reduced police resources lots of stations were closing around the county. The wealthy and influential residents of Leeston would certainly have something to say if they tried to close their local station, though.

For now, Leeston station was a hive of activity as the machinery of the police force pulled together a team to investigate the disappearance of Kelly-Ann Miles. DI Sue Taylor was in charge of the investigation but already there was interest from headquarters and she had to report any progress to her superior officers. This she found frustrating as she had a hundred and one things to do without pandering to headquarters' demands. Why can't they be patient, she thought, there's so much to do setting up and prioritising lines of enquiry? She knew only too well that evidence is best gathered in the Golden Hour, so the decisions she made now would be critical.

When the squad of fifteen detectives had gathered in the incident room, Sue addressed the team. She outlined the circumstances of Kelly-Ann going missing and said, "First of all is there anyone with any ideas or thoughts? Remember, there is no such thing as a bad idea and no monopoly on wisdom." There was silence, so Sue continued, "Right, these are the priority lines of enquiry. The mum has gone home so I want someone to go with the

Family Liaison Officer (FLO) to interview her to get background about her daughter – usual stuff, habits, friends, hobbies, phones. I want a family tree and background checks asap. I want the house searched from top to toe, she may not be there, but there may be clues. I want the eyewitnesses from the park to be video interviewed because they're significant witnesses, but they're children and need to be handled carefully, so trained child interviewers only, please. I want all CCTV from the surrounding areas including shops and garages. Paul, I need a list of possible suspects from your RSOs. Who is capable of this, who could have been planning this? Then prioritise urgent visits on your top ten suspects, you choose them. I need urgent house-to-house enquiries across the estate but prioritise any houses within line of sight to the play park as well as the houses at the other end of the cut-way where they were seen to go. OK, folks, we have to act fast and hard to get her back, we all know her chances of survival reduce the longer we take. So, get out there."

The incident room looked like chaos but was now set up and functioning, information started to flow, and tasks were allocated. Information came in, it was read and evaluated then actions created and prioritised for completion. Sue had a million and one things to do and her mind was buzzing. She had to remain clear-minded and calm for Kelly-Ann's sake, she had to save this little girl. Sue had never met Kelly-Ann, but she and her team were all desperate to make sure that she was safe, and that they were able to get her back. Sue saw Paul Smith still standing in the briefing room with a puzzled look on his face.

"Everything OK?" asked Sue.

"You know, I'm sure I know that girl's name, but I can't think where I know her, it's driving me crazy," said Paul.

"It'll come to you I'm sure, we've got the intelligence team searching all our databases, we might get something from that."

"OK, I'm sure you're right, I'll pull up a list of high-risk offenders for you, but this doesn't match anyone we're currently managing in our area, they may have come from out of area."

"Good point; contact all forces and see if anyone jumps out for this and research similar MOs on the ViSOR computer system." ViSOR was the national database for all known violent and sexual offenders. If someone had a history for abducting children they'd be on the system.

Chapter 15

Kelly-Ann felt groggy, she could only remember bits of what happened, but she knew that she was in big trouble. She was lying fully clothed on a mattress with some smelly blankets strewn on top. Her head was spinning, and she felt sick in her stomach. She knew that she had been with the man from the park, then she couldn't remember anything afterwards. Why was she here – where was here? There was a dull glow reluctantly emanating from a single bare bulb hanging from the ceiling. The room was about the same size as her bedroom but a bit narrower and nothing like her bedroom. The walls were painted a drab grey and the room was musty, lifeless and oppressive. To her right, there were wooden stairs leading up to a door, leading where she did not know.

There was a portable toilet in one corner and a small table with a plastic jug of water and a plastic beaker in another. There was just a packet of stale bourbon biscuits for her to eat but she didn't feel hungry anyway; she felt very thirsty, so she got herself some water. Her world was suddenly very small and empty – but equally very frightening. She had no idea why she was there. Not having anything for reference, she had no clue where she could be, nor what type of room this was, she just knew that she wanted to be home with her mummy and her brother. The thought of home made Kelly-Ann start to cry. If her mummy was hurt she should be with her, why wasn't she with her? The man said he was taking her to her mum.

She realised then that she had wet herself and felt embarrassed, but this was the least of her problems. She cried, then tried shouting but to no avail, she just knew no one could hear her and the room just seemed to absorb her cries. She was really scared, but somehow, she fell asleep, sobbing quietly to herself – confused, lost and alone.

Chapter 16

Sue Taylor was sitting in her office when the phone rang. She could see on the display that it was from the custody sergeant, the person responsible for managing the detention and treatment of people under police arrest.

"Ma'am, I think we've got your man."

"What do you mean?"

"Someone's just been brought in trying to abduct a girl from the same park as your missing girl. I'll send the arresting officer, PC Alison Thomson, up to see you."

Sue hung up and a few minutes later PC Thomson arrived. "Alison, nice to see you, what have you got for me?"

"Have you heard of the Paedophile Hunters?"

"No. Who are they?"

"They're four guys from Swinton, led by Graham Kenny, who go online pretending to be fourteen-year-old boys or girls, depending on their target's interest."

"Sounds dodgy."

"I thought so too, but they then meet men online and get chatting. In no time at all the men initiate sexualized chat and the grooming starts. The Hunters have been well briefed because they don't lead men on, so they can't be accused of being agent provocateurs. They're very good at gathering evidence and their evidence has been used successfully in the past."

"That's interesting."

"The Hunters make it clear to the men that they are fourteen, and eventually agree to meet somewhere for sex."

"Which is a crime," nodded Sue.

"All of this is recorded. The four Hunters then go to the agreed time and place to meet the paedophile. They meet up, all the while video recording their activities. When they find him, they challenge him and make a citizen's arrest. That's when they call the police and that's when I came in."

"Who did you arrest?"

"Damian Paddock, he's not a known RSO. He lives in Lindmouth, we think on his own."

"That's fantastic news, thanks Alison, we'll get right on it. Where are the Hunters? Although I don't agree with vigilantism, I'll reserve judgement until I've seen the evidence."

Sue immediately got onto her DS, Paul Smith, to take over the management of the case. "Arrest him for Kelly-Ann's abduction as well as his current offence and search his place. He must have a car, find it and seize it for forensic examination."

Paul, as always, was efficient and quick. The uniformed patrol officers quickly found Thomson's car, a Honda Civic, which was towed to a secure garage. He got his team to take written statements from the four

Paedophile Hunters and organised a team to search his address.

From trawling through databases, including the internet, the intelligence team discovered that Thomson had been a teacher from Devon but had moved to Lindmouth recently. Some allegations had emerged in his school about sexual activity with two thirteen-year-old girls. He was known amongst staff and pupils to be a bit too hands-on and was heard, by another member of staff, to flirt with the girls and offer to take them out for a drink. Nothing came from the Devon investigation as the girls refused to make a statement, but Thomson had been dismissed from the school and hadn't taught since. Somehow the story had leaked into the local press, so Thomson felt the need to move away from the area.

Thomson lived in a flat near the seafront in Boscombe, there were no sea views, but it was only one road away from the beach and was in a very desirable area. The search team had the keys to the flat. Thomson came with them, and Paul Smith led the search. Thomson was a small, neat man in his thirties with prematurely thinning, fair hair. Walking into the hallway, Paul was immediately impressed by the two-bedroomed flat, which was the upper half of an old character house. The ceilings were high and there was a large bay window in the lounge. The sparse furniture was tasteful and pride of place in the middle of the lounge was an Apple Mac laptop. It was quickly clear that Kelly-Ann was not there, but the next step was to find out if there was any evidence that she'd ever been there. The forensic team moved in, swabbing surfaces, lifting fingerprints and collecting fibres. This was painstaking work, but the Crime Scene Investigators knew only too well how important it was to be thorough.

Throughout the search, Thomson was guarded by an officer to make sure that he didn't interfere with the process. Thomson talked to the officer like a long-lost friend, chatting over facts about his life, his upbringing and interests. Although they'd never met, they discovered a shared interest in ballroom dancing and spoke animatedly about competitions they had entered and mutual acquaintances. This chatter at least made time go by, but Paul thought it strange that Thomson was so relaxed and just said "OK" when he was arrested on suspicion of abducting Kelly-Ann.

Paul Smith couldn't figure Thomson out, either he was the coolest customer he'd ever met or had nothing to hide.

The search took several hours, and the officers seized a number of items of interest: the laptop; several data sticks; the kitchen calendar; three good quality cameras, several long lenses; and a variety of sex toys of differing sizes and shapes. These were in the bedroom cupboard along with a full-sized dog suit. Interestingly the breed of dog was Dalmatian, Paul wondered if this was significant or not. When Paul went through the inventory of items seized during the search, he asked about this unusual costume.

Thomson became animated as he talked about the parties he went to where everyone dressed in animal outfits, then had wild sex together. "An animal orgy, great fun!" Suddenly adding, "All adults, of course!" he explained for clarification.

Paul, although fairly open-minded, thought that Thomson was possibly the strangest man he'd ever met. But did that mean he'd taken Kelly-Ann? No doubt he'd arranged to meet a child, in fact the Paedophile Hunters, for sex but does that make him capable of child abduction – possibly? They all drove back to the station really none the wiser, the laptop should be interesting, though, thought Paul.

Back at the station they all debriefed the day's activity. The car contained nothing of interest and hadn't been seen in the area on the day. It had a comprehensive forensic examination, and fibres were taken which could prove crucial later on in the investigation.

After looking at the evidence gathered by the Paedophile Hunters, Sue Taylor was impressed by the quality and integrity of their work. The video recording of Thomson chatting up and agreeing to meet for sex was undeniable. Thomson led the whole conversation, even double-checking that he was going to meet an underage girl and that they could have sex. Thomson was "bang to rights", in police parlance, on the child grooming case but what about Kelly-Ann? That was the burning question.

Colin, Thomson's legal representative arrived, he was not a qualified solicitor but was a member of a local law firm, colloquially known as a solicitors' "runner". He was a curious character, his natural habitat being the underground cellblock. He had the look of a mole in a suit. Even so, he had a reputation for being straightforward and honest and was a pragmatic realist. Having been given disclosure of the relevant police evidence prior to being interviewed, Colin then took instruction from his client in the interview room. When he came out again an hour later, Colin asked for a chat with Paul Smith.

Colin started, "Look, he's having the grooming but knows nothing about the missing girl. You've got the wrong man there."

"He's got no choice with the grooming offence, but it will go easier on him if he tells us where Kelly-Ann is."

"He didn't do it, granted I can see why you think so, from your point of view, but it wasn't him."

Paul looked sceptical. "Why?"

"The fact is he was out of the country at the time she went missing. Check his passport movements, check with the airline and the hotel. When she went missing he'd gone to Amsterdam for a few days for a sex party in a hotel suite. Would you believe it, about twenty people dress up as animals and have sex in an orgy? They call it "furry cosplay", it's apparently very popular, you know. He's got a cast-iron alibi."

"If you say so, I've seen his costume, a dog… tasteful. But worse than that, I touched it, yuck. OK, thank you, we'll check it out. He's still in big trouble with the grooming, in any case. I appreciate you bringing the alibi to me early on rather than wasting time."

"No problem; just find Kelly-Ann Miles soon, we all know how important time is in cases like this. I didn't want you barking up the wrong tree, if you'll excuse the pun. I've got nephews and nieces, you know."

Paul Smith went through a mental re-evaluation of Colin then got to work. There followed urgent telephone enquiries to prove or disprove Thomson's involvement in Kelly-Ann's abduction. Passport control confirmed that he'd flown to Schiphol airport from Gatwick the day before Kelly-Ann's disappearance.

The hotel was even more helpful, e-mailing the security footage of Thomson's arrival and movements thereafter, showing that he'd spent two nights there. This was conclusive, Thomson could not have done it.

Paul Smith walked tentatively into Sue Taylor's office where she was sitting, poring over the enquiry documents, statements and intelligence reports, trying to extract any new clues or lines of enquiry.

"Sorry to disturb you ma'am, but I thought that you'd like to know about Thomson."

"Well?"

"Thomson did not take Kelly-Ann. He's got a cast-iron alibi, he was in Amsterdam at the time."

"Are you sure?"

"Yes, no doubt, he flew in and stayed at a hotel in Amsterdam for a couple of days. This has all been confirmed and, in fact, he was captured on CCTV."

"So, what now?" Sue looked drained.

Paul sighed a huge sigh, "We'll deal with him for the grooming offence, but we're back to square one with Kelly-Ann. But you know there is still something nagging in my mind, I just can't put my finger on it."

Chapter 17

The following morning Paul launched himself into DI Taylor's office with a look of triumph on his face. "I've got it!" he cried.

"Got what?" said Sue.

"I know where I've heard the name before, the mother of Kelly-Ann Miles was the woman I found with Simon Shaw in the café a little while ago. You know, the one you bollocked me about," he said with a tone of wounded vindication.

"Are you sure? We can't afford to get this wrong."

"I checked my records then popped in to see her. She was distraught when I reminded her about Shaw because she hadn't connected the two events. He's our man, I'm sure of it. I'll get a team together and go and bust him," Paul said with firm conviction.

Sue Taylor was intelligent, quick-witted and decisive. "OK, he's our top suspect for now, get an intelligence package together but it's too risky to just charge in. He might be holding her away from his home, and we may miss our chance to recover her. We'll get a surveillance team on him, he may take us to her. You're in charge of the surveillance, but we need to move quickly, not recklessly. I want to know where he is and what he's doing."

Paul nodded, realising Sue was right, this was one of the reasons why he liked working with her. "We've got the research file already, I'll get a briefing ready for the surveillance team. I already sent someone to watch his house."

"Great, I'll make some calls to get a surveillance authority and get a team here as soon as possible for you to brief. Just so that you know, I'll also do an initial press release, usual thing, police are appealing for witnesses etc. no mention of Shaw, just general stuff." She paused, then said, "Good work, Paul, we'll get her back, I'm sure of it."

Chapter 18

The surveillance team had plotted Shaw's home address, placing themselves in positions to cover Shaw's exit, either on foot or by car. Shaw lived in a small block of flats in an estate at the edge of Leeston town centre. His car, a red 2010 Audi, was parked at the rear of the block of flats but there was no sign of him. Surveillance is all about patience, it is ninety percent sheer boredom and ten percent pure adrenaline-fuelled excitement. The team had to keep on their toes knowing how important the job was. As the day went by, though, Paul Smith lost any confidence that Shaw was there at all. Just as he was about to give up and stand down the operation a call came over the radio, "Stand by, stand by, subject entering The Close, now walking towards the address. He's wearing blue jeans and a brown jacket, he's on foot and alone."

"DS Smith here, all units stay alert, let's see where he's going."

Shaw was closely watched as he walked into the road where his flat was. Where had he been, wondered Paul? Shaw was on his own so Kelly-Ann could be in the flat or somewhere else entirely. What to do next? But instead of going to his flat he got into his car and moved off.

"All units, subject is in his car and moving off towards the main road."

The five surveillance cars all started as one and moved into their well-practiced surveillance formation. They spent the next hour following Shaw as he drove around the Leeston Forest. The word Forest is something of a misnomer, there are trees but mostly it's made up of vast expanses of unenclosed pasture and heathland. The main residents of the Forest are the free-roaming Leeston Forest ponies, these are a distinct breed with an illustrious history going back to 1016 when the Leeston Forest was a Royal hunting ground. There are several small towns and villages that are dotted around its 150 or so square miles – unfortunately for the detectives it also included plenty of remote places to hide a missing child.

What was going on thought Paul, why is he just driving around aimlessly, like a tourist? Does he know we're watching him, is this anti-surveillance, could it be possible that he is that switched on? Having spent an hour keeping a close watch on Shaw, nothing of any real interest happened. He called into his new employers, stopped at a local shop and bought milk. All the time the whole team had to work tirelessly to remain undetected by Shaw, this was particularly difficult in such open areas. They were alive to any indication that he was looking for something, or any clue as to where he may have hidden Kelly-Ann.

As they followed him back home, the static observation post hidden in a friendly flat nearby reported that Shaw had parked his car and had gone into the block. A short while later movement could be seen inside the flat. It was five p.m., it was going to be a long evening for all, thought Paul, as the surveillance cars settled back into their agreed waiting positions. Each car, in turn, took an opportunity to take a natural break and stock up with food. Meanwhile, Paul Smith, not being used to lengthy surveillance and blessed with less patience than the rest of the surveillance team, seethed with frustration.

He phoned the DI for an update and a decision on what to do next, even though he knew what she would say, that they'd have to stay on him at least until the morning and probably into tomorrow. He knew this was the right thing to do, but Paul preferred action, he just wanted to go through the door, then see the look on Shaw's face. The problem is, if she's not there then they could be even further away from getting Kelly-Ann back alive. Paul realised that Shaw would guess they'd be on to him eventually, so must have stashed her away somewhere, but where? Worse still, he could have killed her already and disposed of the body somehow. Either way, he reasoned that it was unlikely that she was in the flat. So, he made the call and his thoughts on strategy were confirmed by Sue Taylor.

As well as watching Shaw, the intelligence unit was busy analysing his phone history. This can often be gold dust in terms of location and call history data. Unfortunately, this wasn't showing up too much of interest except to confirm that he had no friends to speak of, and that he had called several dating agencies over the last three months.

The night dragged on and the smell of stale pizza and unwashed bodies permeated the car. There was no movement from Shaw and with the lights going out at ten p.m., it looked like he was enjoying an early night. Lucky bastard, thought Paul.

For the surveillance team, the morning started obscenely early with the dawn chorus kicking off as the sun came up. The milkman came past on his float, the bottles rattling as he passed. Paul had no idea that they still existed, milkmen seemed like something from a bygone age. He really should be in bed.

Each of the cars and the observation post (OP) were double crewed so that at any one time, one of them was always alert and awake. Therefore, all of them had had some sleep but none of them felt refreshed. They all felt tired and lethargic right up until the point when the OP saw Shaw leaving the flats. "Stand by, stand by, subject leaving the flats and walking towards his car. He is wearing blue jeans and a brown leather jacket again."

Everyone was now on high alert, any thoughts of tiredness now forgotten. They watched Shaw get into his car, then he drove off. Like a ballet troupe, the surveillance cars moved off. They drove so that at any one time one car has the "eyeball" – sight of the subject – whilst the other cars jockey to anticipate where he's going so that they can move into position when needed whilst never being seen themselves.

Once again, Shaw did a grand tour of the Leeston Forest with seemingly no particular aim in mind. Still, Paul thought, was he testing them out, was he that clever? After an hour, Shaw stopped in Blaney–on–Sea and pulled into the Beachcomber Café where he ordered breakfast. The café has wonderful views over the sea and the Isle of Wight, but these were wasted on the surveillance team who had lost their initial burst of enthusiasm when he'd driven away from his flat, to find that he was driving around aimlessly again. After breakfast, Shaw took a very indirect route home but at no time gave any clue as to where Kelly-Ann may be.

After Shaw had gone back into his flat Paul put in a call to the DI to update her on what was happening. "Sue, I'm sorry but we're wasting our time following him, what if she's in his flat?"

"I have thought of that," said Sue testily. "You might be right, though, he doesn't seem to want to take us anywhere she may be hidden. Of course, she may already be dead," she said verbalising what everyone was thinking but didn't want to say. As the senior investigating officer, it was her responsibility to think of all options, even the unthinkable, to dictate the strategic direction for the enquiry.

"Ok," Sue sighed. "Get a warrant and a team together... and you can have the pleasure of busting him."

"Yes, ma'am!" said Paul with real enthusiasm, he'd truly woken up now. He told the team to keep the surveillance on until he came back with an arrest and search team.

Chapter 19

As DI Taylor hung up she saw Joanne James, the acting DS running the house-to-house enquiry team, waiting at the door to her office.

"Hi, Ma'am, can I have a minute?"

Sue rubbed her eyes from fatigue then smiled and replied, "Of course, come in, Jo."

"I thought you'd want to know straight away. From the house-to-house enquiries in Barton road at the back of the park we found the local neighbourhood watch coordinator. She is a thorn in the side of the local police and is worried about people parking in her road to go to the park. She thinks they're all criminals and drug dealers. So, every day she keeps a record of any car that's not local which had been parked there. Over the last month she has a list of twenty cars she says are not residents' cars."

"Great news, we'll raise actions to interview all the owners. Good work."

"It gets better, though. One of the cars is a red Audi registered to one Simon Alan Shaw," said Jo with a huge grin.

Suddenly Sue Taylor's tiredness disappeared. "You're kidding me, that's fantastic, this is just what we need to put Shaw at the scene of the abduction. Wait, was it the day Kelly-Ann went missing?"

"No such luck it was a couple of weeks before. He must have been doing some reconnaissance."

"No problem, I've just authorised his arrest on fairly flimsy evidence, this will help. Was he seen at all?"

"She didn't see anyone with the vehicle, but that probably just means he got out and went into the park. We have found another potential witness, an elderly man who saw someone in a suit near the cut-way on the day. This was likely to be our perpetrator."

"Shaw?"

"We don't know yet, we're interviewing the witness now."

"No CCTV?"

"No, sadly not."

"Don't worry. Jo, please get hold of Paul Smith, tell him the news, he'll love you forever!" Sue joked, not knowing that Jo had a real soft spot for Paul and would dearly love for something to happen between them. Jo blushed, and Sue continued, not noticing her detective's discomfort, "Make sure the car gets recovered for full forensic examination."

Whilst Jo got on the phone to Paul, Sue turned to the task of adjusting and recording her investigative strategy, based on this new information. Although Sue found investigation exciting, it was painstaking work and the paperwork still needed to be done. It also helped Sue by clearly recording any decisions to articulate a clear rationale to make sure that all angles are covered. It's a good self-checking process, if you can't rationalize your thinking, you probably haven't made a good decision. This is an aspect of policing you never see on TV police dramas, thought Sue sourly.

Jo phoned Paul, who, although very pleased with the news, did not profess his undying love for her. Oh well, maybe next time, thought Jo.

Chapter 20

Kelly-Ann woke with a start. She'd been dreaming that she was asleep in her own bed cuddling "Little Bear", her favourite teddy. She slowly realised that she wasn't at home at all and started crying. She sobbed uncontrollably, and her body shook as she did so. She could barely catch her breath and this feeling fed her fear. She felt more alone than she had ever felt before, even more than that day she had been lost in the supermarket. Her mum had been so angry that day and had badly told her off. Would her mum be angry now, would she get told off for going with the man? She missed her mum so much it hurt. She missed her brother, her home, her friends, Little Bear and even school. What would she do to be back at home? She had moaned at her mum whenever she had told her that she had to stay at home, saying it was so boring. If only she could be there now. She'd had lessons about stranger danger, but she'd never believed the message, she thought it was an exaggeration. In any case he knew Mum, so he wasn't a stranger. She so wanted to see her family, even her annoying brother would be a welcome sight now.

She was desperate for a pee, so with some sense of embarrassment she made use of the bucket in the room. She hoped that she wouldn't get into trouble, but what else could she do?

She lay down and tried to think what to do. She had no idea where she was, there were no windows and the only door, which was up a short flight of stairs, was locked. When she first woke up, Kelly-Ann had tried calling for help, but no one came. She assumed that no one was around to hear her. Now she lay shivering and listened intently to try to hear any sign of someone coming to find her.

After what seemed like hours she heard a noise from above. The door shook slightly then opened wide. A face peered in, it was the man from before. She didn't know whether to feel relief or fear. His face was unreadable, and he said nothing, he just left a malt loaf and two apples before closing the door again.

The man returned some time later – was it an hour… or a day? Kelly-Ann had no idea, she had no point of reference, there was no day and no night – just the room.

"Hello, Kelly-Ann." He smiled pleasantly.

Kelly-Ann felt a surge of relief, it was all over he was here to save her, to take her home. She couldn't speak so full of joy was she.

"Hello," he said again. "Is there anything you need, I'm sorry I've got to keep you down here but it's for your own safety."

"Where's my mum?"

"Ah, I'm sorry, but it was worse than we thought, and she has died. We didn't get to the hospital in time, so I bought you here. But before she died she asked me to look after you."

Kelly-Ann looked in shock but said nothing. "I said that I would be happy to care for you, and that is why I have to keep you here to keep you safe. Do you understand?"

"Mum is dead?" Kelly-Ann whispered this as huge racking sobs overtook her. Her body jerked like a marionette being pulled around by an angry child.

The man sighed then continued, "Now, I'm going to have to keep you down here to make sure you're safe. Don't worry everyone knows where you are and it's fine. Your school has said you can have some time off for a while, because of your mum. I'll be back later."

Kelly-Ann was in shock and couldn't speak. Before she could process any information, he had closed the door and had left.

Kelly-Ann did not understand any of this, she cried again, her mum was dead, she was alone and afraid.

Chapter 21

DS Paul Smith stood at the door waiting for the arrest and search team to get into place. This is it, thought Paul. They decided to go in at six a.m. to catch Simon Shaw off guard, even so, Paul felt fully awake and excited.

Paul rang the doorbell then followed it up with a loud knock moments later. There was no immediate answer and Paul was about to order a forced entry when the door opened a crack.

Paul barged the door in suddenly, knocking Shaw backwards and tripping him over. As he fell, Paul lunged forwards jumping on top of him, pinning him to the ground, lifting back his fist as if to punch him.

"Where is she, you bastard?"

Shaw, although not small, looked terrified, but said nothing.

One of the DCs stepped calmly into the hallway and moved next to Paul Smith. "Sarge, you'd probably better nick him and caution him first."

Paul Smith looked blankly at him for a second then said, "Yes, of course. Simon Shaw, you are under arrest for the abduction of Kelly-Ann Miles." Smith continued to caution Shaw, and as he did so he felt his initial fury subside.

He climbed off Shaw, who was ghostly pale and spluttered, "I don't know what you're talking about, I don't know any girl of that name."

Paul stared at Shaw and said through gritted teeth, "You're lying, and I know you're lying because I saw you with her mother. Do yourself a favour and tell me where she is."

For a second Shaw looked in shock, then muttered, "The missing girl is Julie's daughter? I didn't know... I don't know anything about this."

Paul leaned towards Shaw and said, "You'll forgive me for not taking your word for it. OK, everyone, let's pick this place to pieces, there must be some link to where he's taken her." The search team was led initially by a forensic manager – to make sure that any opportunity to retrieve any forensic material was not missed. Even the smallest clue, a hair, fibre or blood spot could be significant and may be crucial in any future trial.

Shaw slumped down on a chair in the living room. He just stared ahead looking intently at some unknown spot on the wall while the search officers systematically and thoroughly dissected the flat, seizing anything that might be relevant.

Shaw said nothing during the search as he saw his life being pulled apart yet again. Inside, his mind was racing, but he was careful to not say anything to antagonise the police, not knowing what they were capable of.

The crime scenes investigators were most excited by blood found in the bathroom and some hairs on the sofa.

Other than those two things there was no sign of anything interesting and the evidence search continued.

The police seized his laptop and phone as well as a number of things that made no sense to Shaw. When the search ended two hours later Shaw was exhausted and was glad that it was over. He was confident that there was nothing to find there, but would they plant something? He was desperately thinking what there was to connect him with Julie's kid. He broke into a cold sweat as he thought what evidence might be found against him, but this time he would say nothing for his own reasons.

When they had finished the search, Paul Smith sat down with Shaw and went through the handwritten record of all the items seized in the search. Shaw agreed with the record made of the search but made no comments about any of the items seized, and the search was closed.

When they opened the door to the flat to leave, Shaw saw that there was a local reporter from the *Evening News* on the doorstep. As they all came out the reporter shouted questions at Shaw asking where Kelly-Ann was, is it true that he was a convicted paedophile, was there anything he wanted to say?

Shaw put his head down and said nothing. Paul Smith seethed at the sight of the journalist and thought about the revenge he would visit upon whoever had alerted the press to their operation. As they went to the cars parked nearby a couple of TV cameras seemed to appear from nowhere. A small crowd had also formed which looked like a rent-a-mob, where do these people come from?

Again, there were questions shouted from the journalists from the various TV stations, one of the journalists Paul quite liked, but they were nothing but a hindrance now. One of the biggest risks with this press activity was that the information would stop coming in from the public about the abduction, because they thought it was now all solved. He knew that they had a job to do but why do journalists behave like vultures, making his job so much harder?

The small crowd of about ten locals had gathered, having been attracted by the TV cameras. They were a real mixed bag of teenagers, the unemployed, mothers and an old man with a small dog. They all glared at Shaw and added their own calls of "pervert" and "paedophile" to intensify the atmosphere. Shaw wondered who had alerted them, maybe it was Smith just to put some pressure on him?

Smith and the rest of the officers looked stony-faced and said nothing as they got Shaw into a car, they quickly packed their things away, then drove off.

Getting Shaw back to the police station was uneventful and when he was booked into custody by the sergeant, Shaw said that he wanted a solicitor as soon as possible and would not speak until he had done so. The custody area was also known as the "Bridewell". Its name was taken from a 16th-century prison in London. It was a grim place. Airless with no windows it had the look, feel and ambience of a subterranean urinal. The place was designed for discomfort. This included the oversized desk raising the custody sergeant several feet above any prisoners, so that anyone coming in had to look up to answer questions.

Shaw had all his personal possessions removed from him, and then he was placed in a cell. The cell was about ten feet square with a small stainless-steel toilet in the corner and a low wooden and steel bed to the side. There was a hatch and a peephole in the grey steel door, so privacy was non-existent.

The worst thing was that this was familiar, a part of him felt safe and comfortable being locked up. The outside world is not an easy place to live in. He forced himself to stop thinking like that, he must find a way out, and quickly. He had things to do.

When the solicitor arrived, he had to think; what should he tell them? He needed to be careful, can they be trusted? His past experience disinclined him to trust lawyers, but he knew that he needed one, as he was way out of depth, and this was truly serious.

Chapter 22

DS Paul Smith finished briefing his interview team. Paul was fortunate that his newest DC, Nick Webb, was a very experienced and advanced trained interviewer. Nick also knew Shaw as he had recently taken on his offender management. Nick knew all about Shaw's connection to the Miles family as this had happened just prior to his arrival on the team. The other interviewer was Ali Mitchell, a DC from the Major Crime Team, who also was very experienced. She was an advanced interviewer and had a good reputation.

Ali was in her early forties, a career detective, who had sacrificed her personal life to the job. She was attractive and impressive, intelligent and astute, the perfect combination of attributes that put most men off, who felt intimidated by her.

Paul told them, "The important thing is to get a good account of Shaw's movements, particularly on the day his car was near the scene and the day that Kelly-Ann went missing. Somewhere within those movements will be a clue as to where Shaw had hidden Kelly-Ann. We need to know about friends, relatives, associates, and any connection with any premises, particularly where she could be locked away. Where does he frequent? Check his movements against where he went when he was being followed. This, of course, is assuming that Shaw doesn't want to make a full and frank confession." Some chance, thought Smith, Shaw was cool and arrogant, this was not going to be easy.

Paul continued, "The priority is to get Kelly-Ann back alive, so try to appeal to Shaw to tell you where she is, tell him it would be easier for him."

Paul summed up, "Shaw is a slippery customer, he's intelligent and cunning. Ali, do not be fooled by Shaw. He will present himself very well and very convincingly. He is devious and evil, he has obviously planned this from the start and will not roll over very easily."

"That's what I don't understand, if he's so cunning and devious why take a child with such an obvious connection to him?" Ali said with a frown.

"Because he is arrogant and superior as well, he thinks he can do anything and we are all too stupid to catch him. It's also the game, the thrill of outwitting the local "plod". He can't help himself," said Paul.

"He certainly is an arrogant bastard," said Nick, who had met him when taking on his offender management.

"OK, well let's see what he has to say. Has he got a brief?" Ali asked.

"Duty solicitor," said Paul with a smile.

"Any good?" asked Ali.

"New," said Paul, "perfect for us."

Ali and Nick then went off together to read all the available information and prepare themselves for conducting possibly the most important interview of their lives.

Surprisingly to Ali, she and Nick seemed to get on really well. They had a similar sense of humour and they seemed to be very comfortable in each other's company. Ali had to remind herself that she didn't date coppers, they were unreliable as boyfriends and mixing home and work was the easiest way to get a bad reputation – still, always a first?

When they had finished their prep, they went to get coffee while they waited for the solicitor to finish their briefing with Shaw.

Chapter 23

"Sorry, but do your parents know where you are?" Simon Shaw sarcastically addressed the duty solicitor who had come into the interview room. Blushing, she introduced herself as Debbie Martin. Probably with a smiley face over the "i", thought Shaw. It didn't help that she wore a blazer, skirt, shirt and tie which looked to Shaw like a school uniform.

Debbie Martin had always been told that she was lucky to look so young but sometimes (like now) she thought it a curse. In fact, she was very bright and capable and had been qualified for several years. Even though she had only recently started on the duty solicitor scheme, she was used to this type of prejudice, and although it annoyed her, she knew how to cope with it.

"Look, no offence, but I want a proper solicitor."

"At the moment, Mr Shaw, I am your only option and the only one standing in the way of you heading to Winchester prison on remand. So please can we just get on with this?"

Shaw was taken aback by the severity and authority of her response and not a little impressed. So, Shaw told his story starting with the circumstances of his original conviction, his meeting Julie for coffee, being exposed by DS Smith in the café and finally his arrest at home.

Debbie looked at him hard. "And what else?"

"What?" said Shaw.

"What are you holding back?" said Debbie staring hard at him.

Shaw looked uncomfortable. "Nothing," he said.

"You'd better try to be more convincing than that when the police talk to you!"

"OK, there is something. I went to see Julie after it had gone wrong in the café, to apologise to her."

"OK, did you see her?"

"No, I didn't get that far. She told me roughly where she lived, the road name and that it was opposite a play park, but I didn't know her address. I walked around but didn't see her, so I left. I don't think anyone saw me and I parked my car away from her road."

"When was this?"

"Some weeks ago, the day after the police barged in on my date, I left that day in a hurry, I wanted to apologise."

"But you never saw her, and no one saw you?" asked Debbie, slowly taking notes.

"Not that I'm aware of."

"In that case, we'll keep that to ourselves for now, it's not up to us to do the police's job for them."

Shaw looked relieved, "If you're sure?"

"Yes, if they find out we'll cover it then. Unless you have anything else we'll give them a written account of what our position is, including your movements on the day in question. Other than that, we'll give no comment until we get more idea from them what evidence they have."

"So, let's go through some detail, what were you doing the day Kelly-Ann went missing?"

"That's the bad news, I'm not sure. I could have been at home but since I've been on my own, I tend to spend time just driving around the Leeston Forest. I love the place, I find it relaxes me and there is no one around to make my life difficult."

"Can anyone vouch for this?" asked Debbie hopefully.

"No, I've become pretty much a loner since my friends and family abandoned me. That's why I try dating sites, I know I need company, really. I'm not a bad person, you need to know this. I made a mistake before, but I paid for that, surely I deserve a chance to show I'm not that person they think I am?"

Debbie and Shaw went through his account in some detail and when it was finished she told the custody sergeant that they were ready for the interview.

"Are you OK?" asked Debbie.

"Let's do it!"

Chapter 24

Ali and Nick walked into the interview room well prepared to try to get a confession from Shaw. Nick and Paul seemed convinced of his guilt, but Ali was not so sure. The detectives both wore serious business suits, obviously designed to intimidate Shaw. Shaw was not easily intimidated, though and it seemed neither was Debbie.

After introductions, all of which were recorded, Debbie said, "Due to insufficient disclosure, my client has prepared an account for you but will not be willing to answer any questions at this time. You have provided no real evidence to justify his arrest, let alone his continued detention."

"That's your opinion, nevertheless we will be asking your client questions," replied Ali coolly, she had come across this tactic before and wasn't completely surprised bearing in mind the grounds for arrest were circumstantial. Still, they had their "ace" which they were keeping close to their chests. Shaw's written account makes no mention of him going near to Julie's address and they hoped to catch him off guard with the information.

They went through all the information on the prepared statement and questioned Shaw to verify his account. On each occasion he said, "No comment."

After about an hour of this Nick threw in, "Have you ever been to Julie Miles' house?"

Shaw looked at his solicitor quickly then said, "No comment."

"Do you know where she lives?"

"No comment."

"Have you ever been to the area she lives in?"

Shaw paused and looked at Debbie, momentarily unsure of what to do, then said, "No comment."

"I should remind you of the caution that explains that it may harm your defence if you do not mention, when questioned, something which you later rely on in court. Do you know what this means?"

Shaw knew exactly what that meant. It was this very problem that he'd previously encountered, by not giving an explanation for his actions before his first trial. The judge told the jury that there was no credibility in anything he said in court because he could have said it before. Back then he had made no comment because the solicitor said so, but was that the right advice now?

Luckily, at that point his solicitor interjected, "I'd like to confer with my client, please?"

Ali and Nick looked annoyed and said, "But there is a line of questioning we want to pursue."

"And a very short conference with my client will facilitate that, I'm sure."

When the detectives had left the room Debbie declared, "They know... my instinct is that they know you've been there, they must have somebody who saw you there. I suggest that we come up with an additional statement clarifying when and why you had gone around to the address. Don't worry, this is not a problem we hadn't already anticipated."

"OK, I'm happy to explain, because it's the truth. Can I answer their questions about this?"

"OK, but don't let them lead you into anything you don't want to say."

"I'm not an idiot." Shaw started to say more but was interrupted.

"And neither are they. Don't make the mistake of thinking you can be clever about this, that sort of behaviour will get you into prison."

The two detectives returned to the interview room and recommenced the interview. Nick started by asking, "OK, we were talking about Julie Miles' house, have you ever been there or to the area she lives in?"

"Yes, I have been to the area she lives in."

"Why?"

"I went the day after your DS Smith publicly embarrassed me. I wanted to apologise to her… to explain my point of view."

"Did you see her?" asked Ali.

"No, I didn't know her exact address. I know she lives near the play park because she told me. I walked about a bit but didn't see her."

"Where did you park your car?"

"In the road on the other side of the park, I was nervous about parking too near her road because the police might spot it and make a fuss."

Nick interjected, "How many times have you been back?"

"Never, I just went there the once."

Nick became aggressive. "You're lying we know you're lying. You were seen on the day talking to Kelly-Ann, where did you take her? Where is she you bastard?"

"I wasn't, I didn't, I haven't…"

"You took her, we know you did, now tell us where she is, it will go easier on you if you do."

"I've never even seen her, let alone spoken to her, I didn't do this."

"We have witnesses who saw you and have identified you."

This revelation was news to everyone in the room and Debbie quickly interjected, "Wait, I haven't had any disclosure about identification evidence! I need to talk to my client."

Nick was flushed, and Ali glared at him, as she said, "No problem at all, will ten minutes be OK?"

When Ali and Nick were away from the interview room she rounded on him, her face red with anger, "What the hell, Nick?"

"What?"

"Why did you say we had identification evidence when we haven't? You can't do that, it's a breach of PACE."

PACE is the Police and Criminal Evidence Act which governs police activities including suspect interviews. Any breach can seriously compromise an investigation and make evidence inadmissible in court. Lying about evidence would be a breach of this Act.

"Yes, but we will have when the witnesses do the identification process. That smug bastard has got her and we need to do whatever we can to get her back. Don't you agree?"

"Yes," Ali said reluctantly, "but we still need to follow procedure."

"Look, what's important is that we find that little girl and that man knows where she is!"

"OK, but no more lies or we'll both be for the high jump."

Back in the interview room, the interview had reverted to no comment, so after another half an hour the interview ended. "I shall be making representations for my client to be released, you have no evidence except what you're obviously fabricating." She looked pointedly at Nick who tried hard not to look back at the lawyer.

Chapter 25

DS Paul Smith and DCs Mitchell and Webb were standing uncomfortably in DI Taylor's office. "What on earth have you been up to? I have been hearing from the custody sergeant that the duty solicitor claims that you are making up evidence, that you lied about the existence of identification evidence?"

Paul responded first, "Look, I'm sorry, we got ahead of ourselves, he will be identified, but it just hasn't happened yet."

"It's my fault…" started Nick.

"I don't care whose fault it is. Look we're getting nowhere with him, and we have no reason to keep him. To save your arses, I've agreed to release Shaw while we complete our enquiries, including conducting an identification parade which you so prematurely introduced into evidence."

Paul started to speak but Sue cut him off, "Don't argue, we're getting surveillance back on him and it may well lead us to Kelly-Ann… if he is involved… of which, I am not entirely convinced. Look, Paul, I know you're certain it's him, but we have to follow the evidence and, like it or not, we simply don't have the evidence yet."

"But I know it's him, I'm sure of it," said Paul. "Remember Occam's razor."

"What?" said Sue, dreading another lecture.

"Occam's razor, the principle that the simplest answer is most likely the correct answer."

"Look, I have no interest in whatever shaving equipment you're currently obsessed with, I need evidence! Find some evidence that we can use in court, that's what we deal with, real tangible evidence! The phone data doesn't even put him anywhere near the scene, looks like he was nearer the other side of the Forest when she went missing, that's miles away."

"At least his phone was!"

"True, but let's work hard and get the evidence, no shortcuts, OK? And we need to be open-minded also. Any questions? Understand that this is a done deal, though, I have smoothed it over with the solicitor on condition that we release Shaw... for now. I have apologised for what happened and that is an end to it."

"No ma'am," all three chorused, seemingly chastened by the experience. He hid it well, but Paul was seething inside.

"Paul, you're with the surveillance team again, brief them to take him off from the custody suite. I want him followed the moment he leaves here with the hope that he'll take us to Kelly-Ann."

Paul Smith nodded then walked away with Ali and Nick. "Look, sorry, sarge, that should have been my bollocking!" said Nick.

"Don't worry, I probably would have done the same – he will be identified, I'm sure of it. The boss is right though, we have to do the work first, following him again is a good option. You two go home, it's been a long day."

Ali had noticeably said nothing, but inside was angry. She didn't agree with either of them, she was upset that she'd been made to look professionally incompetent. She prided herself on having a good reputation and didn't want to be thought of as slipshod and reckless. When Nick asked if she wanted to go for a drink she just coldly replied, "Maybe next time," before striding off towards the car park.

Whilst waiting for the surveillance team Paul went to the office to get a cup of tea, then wandered into the custody area. Paul saw a new, young face behind the custody sergeant's desk. It was an acting sergeant Paul had not met before.

Paul introduced himself then asked, "I hope you've been briefed about Shaw?"

"Yes, of course, I was told that he was to be released subject to investigation, so I let him go about ten minutes ago."

"What about surveillance? He was to be released when we had the surveillance team ready to follow him, not before. Why the hell did you do that?"

"When I was told to release him, it would have been unlawful to keep him in custody; that would be my neck on the block."

"As it is, I'll have your balls on the block for this, you just released and lost our kidnapper! Where is he now?"

The acting sergeant had the grace to look embarrassed. "No idea, he left the back way. I gave him his car back… I was told you'd finished with it."

Speechless, Paul stormed out of the custody area and went to track down DI Taylor. How was he to explain this cock-up? As he started to explain to Sue what had happened, the surveillance team turned up. Too late, thought Paul bitterly. Still, it was not their fault, it was that idiot of a custody sergeant.

Sue was remarkably calm about the whole thing and quickly put in plans to recover the situation. They put observation posts on Shaw's home and work, but in reality, they had no idea where he could be. They'd have to try to track him down somehow. It was at times like this that Sue was at her best, she thrived on pressure, some people fell apart if things went wrong, but Sue came alive. For example, when relationships broke up she wouldn't wallow in self-pity, she'd turn her mind to a new project or hobby, that way her career flourished, and she became very accomplished at what she did. Albeit she was a bit lonely, occasionally, Sue felt that this was a small price to pay for her independence.

Typically, Sue let her staff go way before she left for the night.

Chapter 26

Kelly-Ann was asleep when I got back to the cottage. She looked like she was wrapped lovingly in the arms of Morpheus, where she dreamed of another life long ago, her old life when she was happy. She woke suddenly when the door opened with a squeal.

"Hi, Kelly-Ann," I said. "How are you doing? Sorry I was away so long. I had some things to do."

Kelly-Ann seemed happy to see me but was afraid to say anything. I took her up the stairs into the cottage where I allowed her to shower. I stayed with her to help her with her hair and, although she was initially self-conscious, she allowed me to help. Smelling clean and fresh again I made some food and we sat at the kitchen table to eat together. We chatted about nothing much. Kelly-Ann was reluctant at first then cheered up, feeling safe and secure with me as I successfully groomed her, in no time at all. It's that easy!

"I'm your dad now," I said, "and if you'd like to, would you please call me Dad or maybe Daddy?"

Kelly-Ann thought awhile, then with the simplicity and acceptance of her age she said, "OK."

We cuddled up on the sofa and watched a movie together then I put her back to bed in her cellar. I had cleaned and aired the cellar and replaced the bucket. I told her that because she was in danger, she would have to stay there while I went away to work or wherever. She nodded her acceptance and I smiled broadly at her. "Good girl."

OK, I thought, I've done it she's here, now what? I'll have to be slow and careful, after all there's plenty of time – unless I get caught!

She really was lovely, I can't wait. But the anticipation is the best bit. Still, I don't have to be that patient, she's mine now – she even calls me Dad. I'll look after her, but there will be a bit of a juggle, and I'll need to be careful in case I'm followed. There were outbuildings at the cottage, so I could hide the van away from prying eyes.

I'll need to get plenty of food and water for Kelly-Ann, I'd hate her to starve to death. I'll move a fridge to the cellar, her bedroom, and make it more comfortable, I'll make it a home for her. After all, she'll be here for a while.

I sit in the cottage thinking, I'll need to go home soon. I need to maintain my normal life as well, it will look suspicious if I just disappear. I know very well how difficult it is to live two lives, it's not easy you know.

I drive towards home, conscious that I may have some explaining to do if I'm seen. But thankfully I'm not seen, so all is good.

Chapter 27

Sue was woken up by a call from DS Smith, it was five fifteen a.m. "Boss, he's back home, I've got a team plotted up in case he moves again."

"So what time did he get back?"

"About five a.m., we don't know where he's been though, because we'd already seized his phone."

"OK, he might need to sleep but stay on him in case he moves. I don't care what it costs – we stay on him now until we find Kelly-Ann."

"Sure, boss, I won't let you down again."

Sue said nothing but rang off. Looking around with tired eyes, first light was peeking through her curtains. Her flat was bright, airy and very modern. It was a stylish, waterfront property which was a bit of an extravagance made possible by an agreed cash settlement with her ex-husband. If she'd held out, undoubtedly she could have got more money, but she was happy to accept his first offer and move on with her life. The flat was immaculate and well appointed, all it lacked was any sense of being a home. The flat did not feel cosy; it was comfortable, but it had little furniture and appeared to have even less soul than your average budget hotel. This suited Sue's needs well as she only used the place like a hotel.

A key feature of her life was the absence of a relationship. It's not that she doesn't get offers, but they were usually of the drunken, married variety. No thank you, she thought, that was way too much hassle. She'd have looked online but couldn't bring herself to actually do it; in any case, she might meet someone like Shaw! That would be a nightmare, as poor Julie Miles has found to her cost.

Sue showered, dressed then had her usual breakfast of coffee. Her real pleasure was her bean to cup coffee maker which she'd bought for herself last Christmas. She loved the fresh coffee smell that emanated from her kitchen as she performed the daily ritual.

She drove in her Mercedes the six miles to her office; the car was another luxury she had bought when her husband left. As it was sunny she dropped the roof down to enjoy the air. She definitely wasn't one of those drivers who never take the soft top down, even on glorious days like today. Her drive in was a joy, it was a real pleasure to drive across the Forest to her office. What a beautiful place to work, the wide expanses of open land with ponies, sheep and cattle roaming wild, interspersed by picture-postcard villages and hamlets. Traffic was unusually light, and she got to work quicker than usual.

She took a deep breath as she swiped her card to enter Leeston station by the rear entrance. As she walked the cold featureless corridor to her office the hustle and bustle of the day had started. When she sat down her phone rang,

Sue spent the next hour fielding questions, negotiating over staffing levels and giving advice.

Sue went to the briefing room for the morning briefing. The meeting for all staff pulled all departments together to review what had gone on in the last twenty-four hours and to allocate the work of the day. Sue represented the Criminal Investigation Department and updated the briefing on the missing girl, Kelly-Ann Miles. She told them why they think she'd been taken against her will. She also brought to their attention the identity of the main suspect, Shaw. She asked if anyone had any information about him and the need to report any sightings of him. She said that he was out and about as he was released under investigation. Sue said that even though he was the main suspect they were open-minded about his involvement in Kelly-Ann's disappearance.

The CID investigators were stretched thin; as a rape, several burglaries and a shop robbery had come in for investigation. Despite this, Sue would keep a dedicated squad to investigate Kelly-Ann's disappearance and make some calls to try to get more detectives from headquarters. Sue didn't mention the on-going surveillance operation in case there was a leak. There is the sad reality that someone could be in the pay of the local press to leak stories, so a lot of things had to be on a need to know basis. Someone had told the press of Shaw's arrest, which made life difficult, so she was naturally cautious.

As she opened the door to her office she saw Detective Chief Superintendent Alan "Scotty" Irvine sat at her desk. This was typical of the power games played by this renowned bully, Sue was immediately on her guard. Sue was forced to sit like a supplicant in her own office, whilst Alan leaned back in her chair with a vaguely unpleasant smile on his face.

"So, how's it going, Sue?"

"Fine, sir, very busy at the moment, I have asked HQ for some staffing support."

"You need some help, Sue? I'm glad you think so too. I've asked DCI Steve Jones to take over the Kelly-Ann Miles case, I've appointed him as the Senior Investigating Officer, but you'll be deputy SIO." He looked at her to gauge her reaction, but she wouldn't give him the satisfaction of showing him how upset she was. Sue was ambitious, and this was a statement that she couldn't be trusted with a big investigation.

She calmed herself and spoke slowly, "Can I ask why?"

"Look, Sue, it's not that we don't trust you, but this is becoming high profile and we need to show that we're doing all we can. Steve came in earlier today, he's reviewed your enquiry so far and is briefing the team as we speak."

Sue was astounded at the professional discourtesy; this was a deliberate slap in the face, but she was powerless against this man.

"I'd better get to the briefing then." Sue got up and immediately left the office before DCS Irvine could say anything else. Fuming inside, she thought, he's done this as an intentional snub to get one of his own men in. Steve Jones wasn't such a bad bloke she'd heard, but it was well known that he was favoured by Irvine.

The briefing room went quiet as Sue walked in and Steve looked in her direction. He looked a bit embarrassed as Sue sat down. Sue was angry but not with Steve who she thought was sincere and genuine. "Glad you could make it, DI Taylor. I'm just going through the facts as we know them, to see if anyone has any ideas about anything we've missed. I like to say that there is no such thing as a monopoly on good ideas."

"Really, is that true, anything come up?" said Sue.

The intelligence unit DS spoke up, "Silly season has started, as expected, loads of calls have come in from children saying that various men have tried to grab them. We're following these up but I'm not hopeful. More concerning is that another young girl has gone missing from a play park in Swinton."

"Did this happen after Shaw was released?" asked Sue, hopefully.

"No, he was still in custody at the time, so it definitely wasn't him."

"An accomplice?" suggested DS Smith.

"Maybe, who knows?"

Steve took control. "OK, DI Taylor, can you please go and liaise with our colleagues in Swinton and see if the two missing girls are linked. If they are, we take their job on as well. I think Shaw is a good suspect but the evidence against him is only circumstantial, we need to better research other offences of this kind and maybe pull in a profiler. We can't put all our eggs in one basket, we need to be open-minded. This second disappearance means it could well be someone else entirely. We had one crack at

Shaw and that didn't go well." He glanced sideways at Sue.

Sue couldn't disagree but was conscious of the slight on her competence. Although she resented being usurped in this way, she resolved to get on with it and work along with Steve. Sue had met Steve before but didn't really know him, although he had a good reputation and she was prepared to give him a chance. At least he's good looking and not too old, she managed to smile to herself.

Steve was still talking, and the squad of detectives put forward their theories and thoughts. Then finally DS Paul Smith spoke. He forcefully espoused his firmly held view that Shaw was their man and they needed all their resources directed towards him to prove it. DC Nick Webb supported his DS, pointing out that Shaw is an arrogant narcissist; he's a rule-breaker as well as a convicted paedophile. Nick pointed out that Shaw knows the family, and his car has been seen at the scene of the crime. All the evidence pointed at Shaw – it must be him, he insisted!

Steve listened with equanimity, and courteously thanked Paul and Nick for their input. "Thanks, everyone. Sue, you and I need to talk. Can we go to your office, please?"

When they arrived, Scotty Irvine had thankfully left. Steve immediately sat down in the visitor's chair in Sue's office and watched as Sue sat behind her desk – nothing like his mentor, DCS Irvine, thought Sue, disproportionately pleased.

"Look, I'm sorry about this, Sue, this wasn't my idea. I don't want to tread on your toes, this is still your enquiry but I'm hoping we can work together?" Steve looked a little uncertain, almost nervous.

Sue found this a bit charming but wasn't going to let him get away with it that easily. "I've been running with this from the outset, I've invested a lot in this and I want to see it through."

"Of course, I've no intention of side-lining you. HQ felt you needed support, though."

"HQ or Scotty Irvine?"

"They're the same thing, you know that."

"What we need are more DCs."

"I've got ten DCs en route as we speak."

Sue relented slightly. "OK, thanks, but we need to get on with the job, and there is a lot to do."

"What do you think of the suspect, Shaw?"

"He's undoubtedly arrogant and he has met Kelly-Ann's mother, but I'm not so sure about him, the evidence is very circumstantial."

"Your DS and offender manager seem convinced?"

"Paul is very passionate about his work," stated Sue.

"But not always objective enough?"

"Well, I'll let you make your own mind up." Sue smiled, and they both seemed to relax.

"Are you OK checking out the Swinton abduction?"

"Of course, I'll keep you posted," she said as she left.

Steve spent the next few hours going over the evidence, writing investigation policy and setting and prioritising lines of enquiry. Steve agreed to maintain surveillance on Shaw but was keen to make sure that all other enquiries had moved on. They got lucky with Shaw's vehicle being seen near the scene but what about the vehicles seen on the day of the abduction?

Sue returned early afternoon with news from the Swinton abduction. "Dead end, I'm afraid. The girl in Swinton was found at the estranged husband's address, there is absolutely no connection between the Miles family and their family."

"OK, well thanks for looking into it… I've been thinking, what about the nosey neighbour list of vehicles seen on the day?" said Steve.

"I'll chase up the action manager. I agree we need to stay focused, the vehicles seen on the day should be a high priority."

There was no useful update on Shaw, he hadn't moved from the flat, no doubt planning his next move.

Nothing of any forensic significance was found in the car or the flat but, as per the aphorism "the absence of evidence is not evidence of absence". Also, everyone is so much more forensically aware nowadays thanks to CSI television shows. People know how to cover their tracks far more than was the case in the past.

This was frustrating for Sue, though, she desperately wanted some evidential link between Shaw and the crime. Even though they were still unsure about Shaw, they were investing an awful lot of resources in him, and they couldn't afford to keep this up forever.

The rest of Shaw's phone data came back from the phone provider, his phone was the other side of the Forest when Kelly-Ann went missing, but there is no guarantee he was with the phone. The data showed that on other days Shaw drove a lot around the Leeston Forest. In particular, he spent time in known beauty spot car parks, was this cause for suspicion?

Steve and Sue pored over the statements from various witnesses, looking for missing evidence, but nothing obvious sprang out at them.

Steve had arranged a press appeal and had asked for Julie Miles to speak. When Steve met Julie, he was impressed by this lady. She looked distraught but hadn't fallen apart, she spoke well, and he knew she would go down well on TV. Sometimes it was fraught with danger putting relatives in front of a camera, particularly if it was found later that they were involved with the disappearance in the first place. Neither Sue nor Steve had any such concerns and the press briefing went off smoothly. Sue was also impressed by Steve who spoke sincerely and confidently, fielding questions like a pro but not coming across as too glib. Sue knew that she couldn't have done half as well and was grateful to Steve for being there.

By the time they were finished it was getting late. Staff were all busy, there were no more briefings scheduled so Steve, trying to sound cool, suggested, "Do you want to grab a bite to eat?"

Sue paused, wondering what he was asking, was this an offer of a date or just a practical suggestion about eating food? Sue replied, "OK, where do you fancy?" She found herself a little bit excited about the prospect, after all it's not every day she goes out to dinner with a handsome man – well rarely these days, in fact.

"How about the Italian restaurant in Leeston, Giorgio's?"

"Good," said Sue, safe option, she thought, not fancy but nice food and a relaxed atmosphere.

They drove together in Steve's car, an old Toyota, even though it was only half a mile away at the other end of town. The car was dirty and untidy. Clearly, cars weren't his thing, thought Sue.

The restaurant was quiet and felt intimate and friendly. The staff were attentive but not intrusive. Sue had been here several times, but she was surprised to find that Steve apparently knew the owner, Giorgio.

Having ordered their starters and main courses, Steve explained that he had met Giorgio some years ago when he had been first setting up the restaurant. Giorgio had been the victim of a complex fraud by someone pretending to be an investor. Steve had brought in the perpetrators and had recovered £20,000 cash for Giorgio. This was a third of the stolen sum, but Giorgio was extremely grateful to recover any money at all, and so was always pleased to see Steve.

The evening went very well for both of them and there was an obvious attraction between them. Sue loved Italian food and enjoyed the range of courses from the "antipasto" through to the "dolce". Conscious of work, they shared a bottle of San Pellegrino water. After coffee, they were both feeling very relaxed in each other's company and when the bill came there was no awkwardness as they split it equally.

"My treat next time," smiled Steve.

"Next time?"

"I hope so."

"I'm not tired, do you fancy another coffee at my place? I live near the marina," said Sue.

"Another coffee would keep me awake all night..." He paused. "OK, I'd love to."

They drove round to Sue's flat, parked up, then walked towards the door to the flats. A tall, slim man in dark clothing stepped out of the shadows, startling them momentarily.

"Got a new boyfriend already, Sue?" said the man.

"James, what are you doing here?"

"What's going on?" said Steve.

"This is my ex-husband, who should not be here."

"Husband, we're not divorced yet."

"It can't come soon enough," she countered. "Anyway, what are you doing here?"

"Just passing by, and just as well by the look of it."

"This is a work colleague, we're on a case," said Sue.

James smirked. "Looks like you're hard at it."

Steve bridled and stepped towards James aggressively. "Look I don't know what your game is, but you'd better clear off now."

"Or what?"

"Or I'll arrest you for harassment," said Steve, showing his police warrant card.

James hesitated, he was a bully and used to getting his own way. "OK, I'll leave you two love-birds. I wonder, is this professional misconduct? I'll check with my lawyer," he said as he sauntered away, trying to look casual, wanting the last word.

"Tosser," said Steve after he'd gone.

"Sorry about that," said Sue looking sheepish. "We've been separated for a year, but he won't let go."

"I don't want to lecture you, but there are things you can do, advice you can get."

"I know, I'm a terrible hypocrite, but it's not that easy you know."

"I know. Look, let's call it a night, I'll just walk you to your door."

"Are you sure? Thanks. Maybe coffee next time?" said Sue with a tired smile. Seeing James here had thrown her. He still had the ability to intimidate. Sue was impressed with Steve's understanding and sensitivity. She found she was growing fond of Steve.

They said goodnight and Steve decided to call into the station before going home. As he walked into the squad room he saw it was mostly empty, apart from two of the analysts who were double-checking statements against actions tasked for completion.

One of the administrators, Sally, looked up with excitement in her eyes. "Boss, I think I've got something. We've been tracking down vehicles seen by the neighbourhood watch coordinator on the day of the abduction. Most check out fine but one of them, a white Renault van, was recently registered under a false name and address."

"Go on," Steve said.

"The name of the registered keeper is Nicholas Humbert, but the address given is an empty car lot in Dorset, I've had it checked. There are no Humberts on our databases."

Steve interrupted, "Ha, clever, Humbert is the main character in *Lolita*, the infamous Nabokov novel. It's about the man who marries a woman he hates, to get access to her fourteen-year-old daughter. It's like a paedophiles' handbook."

Sally continued, "The vehicle also has no insurance or tax. The good news is that we have a report that it was recently involved in failing to pay for fuel at a local garage."

"Was that followed up, was anyone arrested?" asked Steve.

"No, sir, the garage phoned back a short while later that night saying the owner had returned and paid, so we just closed the incident with no action being taken."

"Damn," said Steve, "that could have cracked it wide open!"

"All is not lost, here's the good news," said Sally. "The garage has an excellent CCTV system, I know because we've had CCTV from there before."

"So where is the CCTV footage?" asked Steve, impatiently.

"That's another slight problem we can't get it until 0900 tomorrow, the company has to get it off their server which apparently can only be done when their head office opens."

"OK, I want someone there to get a copy at 0900 then get back here for ten thirty for an all-squad briefing. I want everyone to see the footage at the same time, if it's Shaw at the garage then we've got him, if it's not Shaw then someone may know them!" Steve announced.

This was an unusual approach, but Steve seemed to have a flair for the dramatic and clearly wanted to share in the successful find. Sally got busy sending messages to the investigative team, informing them about the following day's early briefing for all staff.

Steve texted Sue with the update and said that he would pick her up at 0800, ending the message with an "x".

Chapter 28

Kelly-Ann woke up, sharp and alert, as I came down the stairs and sat next to her. "Hi, Kelly-Ann, how are you?" I say as I put my arms around her.

She stays still, trembling very slightly, but says, "OK, thank you."

"Look, I've adopted you, I'm now your daddy, so I thought I'd let you choose a new name. What name do you want to be called?"

"Kelly-Ann, that's my name," she said, studying her feet.

I squared up to her and put my face close to hers, I spoke forcefully so that she would understand, "Look at me. Daddy, you call me Daddy!" How could she be so ungrateful? She flinched and tried to pull away from me. I pulled her closer again, then said more soothingly, "I know it's been tough for you, but you're safe with me now. You'll be getting a new life from now on, so there must be a new name you'd like."

She seemed to think for a long time then, just as I was losing patience, whispered through her tears, "I like Crystal."

I looked hard at her, "Daddy. Say Daddy."

"Crystal, please, Daddy, can I be Crystal?"

"Crystal, it is, I like it." I beamed at her, and she smiled back uncertainly. I gave her a long hug and said, "There's a good girl, Crystal, now don't forget your new name and be a good girl, you never know, we might go outside again… but only when it's completely safe."

I spent the next half hour stroking her arms and legs and making her calm and safe. We chatted about nothing and I told her stories, the few that I could remember that Helen had told me when I was young before she left. We have such a lot of time to look forward to together, it is no use rushing things, she's now mine, she is completely cut off from her past, she only has one future, one option and that's with me.

Chapter 29

Steve and Sue arrived early to prepare for the briefing. The officer tasked to collect the DVD from the garage had not yet arrived, but a message had been sent that he was on his way, having collected a copy of the DVD from the garage.

The room filled as the whole squad turned up. There was excited chatter about the rumour of a new lead, but no one could guess what it could be.

At last the uniformed officer with the DVD turned up and handed it to Sue. "Ma'am, here's the copy of the CCTV."

Sue loaded the DVD into the computer and fired up the projector. Steve started the briefing by giving everyone an update as to where the investigation was at that point. "Now I'll hand you to DI Sue Taylor who will reveal what we hope to be a major breakthrough."

"As you all know a local neighbourhood watch coordinator is in the habit of recording any non-local vehicles parked in the area in case they are there to burgle houses. From tracking down vehicles recorded at the scene on the day of the abduction we found one recently registered to what we think may be a false name and address; a Renault van registered to a Nicholas Humbert at a non-existent address. He's got a sense of humour because this is the name of the main character from *Lolita*, a novel about child abuse. He'll need it, because luckily for us there was a recent incident at Leeston garage involving the van and we think the driver has been caught on CCTV. I have here the first viewing of the DVD, just arrived from the garage, which DCI Jones and I wanted to share with you as soon as we could."

Sue heard a door slam from the corridor behind but thought nothing of it. Enjoying the moment, she said, "These are the first pictures of our suspect, and the biggest lead yet in this enquiry." Out of the corner of her eye she saw Paul Smith writing something in block capitals. Sue started the DVD player then sat down. Looking over Paul's shoulder she saw the words OCCAM'S RAZOR written in capitals on the sheet of paper. Smug bastard, thought Sue, smiling to herself.

The footage showed the van pulling up onto the forecourt of the garage. The driver got out but there was a collective groan in the darkened room when the driver faced away from the camera and couldn't be seen. The person, wearing dark clothing filled up. Again, the driver was facing away from the cameras as he walked to the cashiers. Then the CCTV switched to the inside of the garage and everyone could clearly see the face of the driver walking into the shop then up to the counter. There was a collective gasp, and a variety of expressions of confusion and amazement. Sue scanned the room frantically but obviously couldn't see what she was looking for. "Where's DC Webb, where's Nick Webb."

"He left just before the video started, ma'am, he said he had an urgent appointment."

"I bet he did!" For there on the screen was the crystal-clear image of DC Nick Webb standing in the garage, waiting to pay for the fuel. He was the driver of the van, he was Nicholas Humbert, unbelievably the kidnapper could well be one of their own.

"Get him back now, don't let him leave!"

There was scuffling as there was competition to get after Nick. Sue spotted Paul looking perplexed, screwing up his sheet of paper looking less smug than he had before. Paul then ran for the exit.

Sue and Steve formed a quick huddle. "Well, I wasn't expecting that!" said Steve. "What do we know about Nick Webb, apart from the fact that he obviously knew he was about to be exposed and has gone on the run?"

"Clearly, we don't know nearly enough, I'll get some research going," said Sue. "This does make more sense though; Nick Webb knew Julie Miles because he was managing Shaw. He must have thought it was a good opportunity to stitch Shaw up for it as well... and we fell for it. I should have looked into Webb a bit more when he transferred."

"Don't blame yourself, nobody suspected him," said Steve.

At that point, Paul and other members of the team came back in. "He got away, I've circulated his car registration by radio and flagged it on the computer in case he's spotted."

"Great, we need someone to go to his home address, I can't imagine he'd go there but we need to search it, also get an urgent trace on his phone," said Sue.

"What about Shaw?" said Paul.

Steve answered, "He's no longer our priority. Stand down the surveillance on him, this is now a manhunt for Webb. Unless anyone disagrees, we now have Nick Webb as our priority suspect."

Sue looked at Paul, but no one argued, and the machinery of the investigation shifted in an entirely different direction.

Webb had not yet been caught, he had switched his phone off to avoid being traced, but they got lucky. Webb's car had been caught on a traffic camera heading on the main A35 heading towards Lindmouth.

"Right, get on to a Lindmouth link, I need CCTV and I want to know about anyone he knows there, I want any known addresses visited and checked out."

Chapter 30

Pulling out of the police station car park, I thought, OK, that was bad luck. Damn that garage, why did I forget my wallet, why did they contact the police? I told them I was getting the money. Still, I said that I was lucky. It was my good fortune that nobody viewed it before I had a chance to get away. What now, though? My plans will have to change… what to do? They're so stupid they'll never catch me, but can I take Crystal with me? She's mine now, surely, I've got to try to get away with her. It's either that or leaving her to die in the cellar. I need time to think. I got rid of the phone straight away, so I can't be tracked, but now I need to get rid of the car.

I deliberately drove at speed past an Automated Number Plate Recognition camera on the A35 to make it look as if I was heading into Dorset. I then doubled back into Leeston and stopped to get a hire car. At the railway station, I parked my car undercover in a long-stay car park and paid for five days. I then walked to the nearest car hire company.

Because I'm cautious and clever, I always have a "go bag" in the car in case things go wrong. The bag is in case of an emergency like now and contains some clothes, money and false bank and identity documents. I have always planned ahead and have always been ready to run if needed.

In the car hire office, I chose a mid-range, unobtrusive car, a grey Ford Focus – something anonymous, something like me, a "chameleon" car, remembering what that idiot Smith said about blending in. Ha, what did the pompous fool know about deception? I handed over my fake driving licence and bank card to the receptionist. I got in the car which I had hired for five days so as not to attract attention, not that I had any intention of returning it, but it gave me time to leave the country. I then drove slowly and carefully back to the cottage to see Crystal, maybe for the last time.

I pulled onto the drive with butterflies in my stomach, what was waiting for me there? I know no one can possibly connect me to this address, but I was still nervous. After all, even the best-laid plans can go wrong, who knew that better than me?

I opened the door, there was no sign that anyone had been here. I made myself a strong drink, a single malt scotch, maybe a bit early but, who cares? I needed a drink to steady my nerves, then when I had stopped shaking, I went to see Crystal with a smile on my face.

As I went down into the cellar I said, "Hello, Crystal."

She smiled back and dutifully replied, "Hello, Daddy."

"Come up with me to have some dinner, we should have some special time together."

We both climbed up the stairs, I had poured Crystal a bath with lots of bubbles, and she shyly took off her dirty clothes. She had a long bath until the water went cold, and I helped her wash her hair. Having wrapped her up in a thick, fluffy dressing gown we sat down in the kitchen. We chatted while I cooked a simple tea of fish fingers and chips. She devoured the meal as though it was the best meal ever and I could visibly see her spirits lift.

"I thought we could watch a movie together, I've got *Frozen*."

She smiled, and we snuggled up on the sofa to watch. What a crap film, I thought, at the same time as pretending to love it as much as her. I carefully accustomed her to my touch by gently stroking her arms during the movie. This was really one of my favourite times, it was like hunting or fishing, being patient, careful and cautious, slowly building her trust.

It was mid-afternoon when the movie ended but all the curtains were closed and, because she had been locked in the cellar, time had no meaning for Crystal. I said, "Come on, Crystal, you can sleep in my bed, I think you're safe enough now."

She smiled and nodded, and we went into the bedroom together. I thought that this better be good, Crystal, your life depends on it.

Chapter 31

Steve and Sue were getting a briefing on progress made by Paul Smith. They were in Sue's office and were drinking coffee to keep themselves alert. Along with the rest of the squad they'd been working around the clock. While this was OK as things were happening, and adrenaline was pumping, there is a huge energy crash when it slowed to nothing, like now. It seems Nick Webb had no close friends; his flat was sparsely furnished and sterile. There were very few personal items and, more importantly, no clues as to where he may have gone. His phone was dead, and the car had disappeared. Things were not looking good.

"We're still doing background checks, but the most disturbing thing is what I've just been told by his last boss," said Paul.

"Go on," said Steve.

"Well, Nick told us that he'd volunteered to move to our department for a change of scenery. That was not true. It seems that the truth is much more sinister. Nick was, in fact, being investigated for what they called inappropriate contact with witnesses. He'd met and formed a relationship with two witnesses during investigations he was involved in. Both of the women had daughters, but one of them complained to her social worker that Nick was getting a bit too familiar with her eleven-year-old daughter. The social worker complained, there was an investigation and the whole relationship thing came to light."

"What do you mean, too familiar?" asked Sue.

"He'd volunteered to babysit one night so that the mum could go out with friends. While she was out, he helped her take a bath, washing her hair for her. They said that there was no evidence that he'd indecently touched her and because there was no evidence of any actual sexual assault, there was no criminal investigation. In any case, it was still felt that he should be moved on to avoid embarrassment."

Sue was astonished at what Paul had uncovered. "You mean he was a suspected grooming child sex offender who was moved to a team managing sex offenders, and without us even being told about it? Why am I still shocked? I shouldn't be surprised; how many times have we come across institutional cover-ups?"

"Too often," agreed Paul.

"Was it investigated by specialist trained investigators, or were the children even spoken to by child abuse trained interviewers?"

"No, they weren't, their mums were asked to talk to them," said Paul.

"It gets worse, like they'd confess anything to their own mums! Well, let's add them to our investigation and see where that takes us. Also, we need to speak to any other witnesses he had contact with to see if there is anything else lurking in his past. I bet we'll find a pattern of concerns which have all been ignored." Sue was thinking quickly. "So why didn't they tell us when he moved here, was it a deliberate cover-up?"

"It's more likely to be simple incompetence, is my guess," said Paul.

"Which idiot decided that this was a good idea?"

"Detective Chief Superintendent Irvine apparently. As I said, I think Nick was a bit of a favourite of his."

Steve chipped in at this point, "Look, what's done is done, this isn't getting us anywhere, let's concentrate on finding DC Webb. So, we have a last sighting heading towards Dorset. Any news on friends and associates in the area?"

Sue shot Steve a disapproving look. Was Steve part of the same boy's club? Who knew what connections they may have? Still, it was probably incompetence as Paul said, rather than a conspiracy.

Paul continued. "It seems he has no close friends. He has had a lot of online contact with people we think are abroad, who we are looking at through CEOP." The Child Exploitation Online Protection agency is the country's governmental team set up to deal with online paedophile activity. They also work closely with similar organisations all around the world. If Nick was a networking paedophile then they should be able to identify his contacts. Nick had tried to delete the content from the laptop in his home, but the forensic computer examiners had managed to unlock it and examine the hard drive. They found no indecent images at all, not even adults, which was unusual, but if

Nick was clever he'd be likely to use the darknet, making the activity untraceable.

Sue told them that she had been given the last address he lived in when he joined the police. It looks like he had lived with his dad on one of the large Swinton council estates. Sue said she was going with one of the DCs to ask some questions in the area. There may still be a connection with him, and in the absence of anything better, this was worth a shot. Sue was feeling desperate to do something and felt claustrophobic in the station, particularly as she had unanswered questions about how Webb could remain undetected. How could he have operated right under their noses, was it conspiracy or incompetence? It was only by sheer luck that they had identified Webb as their suspect. What they needed now was another piece of that luck to discover where he was hiding out. The fact that he was a police detective and understood their methods made life even harder.

Steve and Sue agreed that a press release naming Nick would be necessary to shake things up a bit and put him on the back foot. Steve said that he'd go to the media with Nick's picture telling them that he was a suspect in Kelly-Ann's disappearance. "We'll recruit the public to track him down."

The meeting ended, and they went their separate ways, with just one thought on their minds, to save Kelly-Ann Miles.

Chapter 32

Sue drove to Swinton with acting DS Jo James but, even though she liked Jo, she was in no mood to chat. Her mind was filled with dark thoughts and conspiracy theories involving Nick. Should she have noticed something about him, what did she miss? But he just seemed so normal, he certainly didn't look suspicious in any way. They drove into the estate and she observed the scale of uniformity and sameness of the estate. She saw the need after the war to supply plentiful housing, but they could have included some design flair, and just a little imagination to make it look good. Instead, the area was bland and drab and felt depressing as she drove in.

They found the address where Nick used to live with his father. It was a small terraced house with a recently painted blue door. They rang the bell. The man who answered the door said that they'd only just moved there and hadn't known the previous tenants. He suggested they try some neighbours who'd been there longer. Sue knocked at the first neighbour's door which was answered by an older woman who was dressed in very drab grey trousers, a grey blouse and a grey cardigan. When Sue said that they were making enquiries about Nick Webb the woman's face went ashen, as grey as her clothing, she seemed to be rooted to the spot.

Sue, realising that they were on to something, continued. "I understand that he used to live next door to you with his father?"

"He killed my Mickey," she said blankly then motioned for them to come in. In spite of their initial foreboding, the house was clean, neat and tidy, and Mrs Williams was polite and helpful, if a little severe.

She talked of the 1970s when the Webb family lived next door and how that "slut of a homewrecker" had stolen her husband from her, leaving her to bring Mickey up on her own. She spoke of the strange Webb boy, Nicholas. She suspected that Nicholas used to torture and kill small animals in the area. There were rumours, but nothing was proven because a spate of these happened around the time of the marriage break-up. Her own cat, a beautiful tabby called Mr Wiggles, disappeared one day only to be found dead at the bottom of the garden with its stomach cut open. Mrs Williams had no proof that it was Nicholas Webb, but she was convinced in her own mind that it was him, and she refused to speak to, or even acknowledge any of the family again.

The Webb boy was banned from their house, but neighbours reported seeing him hanging around Mickey. He was a strange boy, about twelve years old in 1971, a couple of years older than her Mickey. Her son was told not to see him, but Nicholas seemed to hold Mickey in some sort of thrall. Mickey's behaviour deteriorated, as did his appearance, he lost weight and became generally disinterested and listless. Once a friendly, popular and active boy, Mickey started to argue with her (which he never did) and one day during an argument, lashed out slapping her on the side of her face. She was stunned and angry and said things she would later regret, grounding him for a week.

The following day she came home ready to make things up with Mickey but instead found his lifeless body hanging in his bedroom. The police said that he had tied a nylon cord to the top of the wardrobe and dropped to the floor strangling himself. Mrs Williams refused to accept this and insisted that the Webb boy must have been involved, but the police ignored her and refused to even talk to that evil monster. No note was left, so they would never really know why it had happened. Mrs Williams told them that the Webb boy always looked at her wearing a smug, knowing smile on his face, as if deliberately taunting her.

When the father died she said that the boy, although no longer a boy, was evicted by the council and she'd never heard anything of him since... until now. She certainly wasn't surprised that he was in trouble, she'd tried to tell the police that he must have been involved in Mickey's death, but they just wouldn't take her seriously. They ignored her complaints and finally, at the inquest, the coroner made a judgement that Mickey had taken his own life. She just could not believe that of her beautiful son who had a bright future and so much to live for.

Chapter 33

Shaw was up early making breakfast when he received the strangest call. DS Smith had phoned telling him that he should not worry about anything, that there had been developments and that he should watch the morning news. Smith wouldn't say any more, but he said that they'd be in touch soon.

Confused but curious, Shaw had quickly turned on the morning regional news programme. Following the piece about the perils of dive-bombing seagulls near the seafront, Shaw saw DCI Steve Jones making an appeal for information about DC Nick Webb and Kelly-Ann Miles. It seemed that the police are now of the belief that Nick Webb had taken Kelly-Ann. What the hell was going on? As much as he wanted to be cleared himself, he found it hard to believe what he was hearing. The police talked about two vehicles they wanted sightings of, a dark blue Vauxhall and a Renault van. Nothing much was said but they showed pictures of them both, then explained that there was a belief that they may have already gone to the Dorset area.

Shaw brightened up considerably at this unexpected news, does this mean he's now off the hook? He couldn't quite believe it, but he hoped so, he just desperately wanted to move on with his life.

Today was a work day and, for the first time in a very long while, Shaw was looking forward to the day ahead. He was grateful for the call from DS Smith, but he still had a kernel of bitterness in his stomach when he thought of what they'd put him through. He'd carefully nurtured this bitterness and wasn't quite ready to give this up.

The day at work was interesting and he found that he got on well with his work colleagues. To be honest, it was just nice to work again and have some normal human contact. At the end of the day, Shaw was upbeat and smiled as he said goodbye to his new work colleagues. As he got in his car, though, he thought of the emptiness waiting for him at home. Home, it wasn't really a home, was it? Just a drab, soulless flat – nothing like his home, nothing like the real life he'd once had before he threw it all away. Yes, that was the real truth, he'd thrown it all away himself. It wasn't anybody else's fault, but his own. He alone had done it to himself and now it was up to him to turn it around.

He decided to do what he loved most, now that he was on his own, Shaw went for a long drive around his favourite beauty spots in the Leeston Forest. The peace and beauty of the Forest calmed his mind and filled his soul with the sheer wonder of such magnificent natural spaces.

Chapter 34

I woke up early, but Crystal dozed on. I made our breakfast –last night was nice, I really can't give up now, but we need to get away. I heard the news, now everyone will be on the look-out for us. It's only a matter of time 'til someone spots me or comes to the address for some reason or another. Of course, I have a plan. My idea is to get to Southern Ireland then find a way to Europe, I like the idea of Spain or Portugal. I have cash and money in false accounts, so I should be OK for a while. Then I can get a job and we'll live together, a perfect life as father and daughter. Crystal is already tied to me and will behave as we travel. And if she doesn't behave… well, so be it.

Crystal woke up slowly. "Good morning, Crystal," I say lovingly.

"Good Morning, er, Daddy." She smiles uncertainly, but she is keen to please me.

"Crystal, we're going travelling today. I have bought you new clothes and I need you to be good." I say this while I pack our luggage. I carefully fold and pack a suitcase for each of us. The only thing lacking are travel documents for Crystal. I can try to get some but that's more risky now that I am Britain's most wanted. If the worst comes to the worst, I will smuggle Crystal onto a ferry in the boot of the hire car.

"Where are we going, Daddy?"

"To a wonderful new life, where you can make friends and go to school."

"What about my brother or my old friends?"

"You won't be seeing them again, we're leaving today."

"Oh."

I had hidden the car out of sight and I was convinced no one knew about the cottage, but still I was on edge. I needed to get away, but I knew it would be safer to travel after dark. I'd have to abandon the cottage, so much for my inheritance, but things don't always go to plan!

My stomach lurched as I saw a man walk up the drive towards the front door. He was casually dressed but that didn't mean he wasn't from the police.

I told Crystal to be quiet. I hid down while trying to see what he was doing, I daren't open the door in case I was recognised. It looked like he was carrying a package, he could be a delivery driver, but I hadn't ordered anything, and the police often used this ruse to see if anyone was at home. I stayed down while he looked around looking undecided about what to do. After a while, he walked towards the road with the package. When he was out of sight I thought that we need to get out of here tonight.

Chapter 35

It was early morning, but the enquiry team was already hard at work. The press release had been a huge success in terms of information and sightings coming into the enquiry room. The downside was that there was too much information, there were sightings almost from Land's End to John O'Groats and all places in between. The real skill was to prioritise the best leads. This was not, however, an easy thing to do. All the enquiry teams were at full stretch chasing down the most credible sightings.

The call handlers had taken one call, though, which had caused some excitement.

"We've had a call from a member of the public who saw a man looking like Webb dragging a girl into a remote cottage. In the right area for us, as well, I think. The witness saw this in passing as he was out cycling and only realised that this was important when he saw the late news. Apparently, the witness is a local GP and hadn't seen the man or girl at the cottage before. It seems the cottage has only been recently occupied again." Steve Jones was talking to Sue whose eyes lit up at this news.

"We need a team there now!" said Sue.

"They're already there, I'm waiting for an update."
Steve's mobile rang, "They're at the door, there's no reply,
they're asking for permission to force their way in."

"Yes, yes!" said Sue.

"Let's hope," said Steve.

Chapter 36

DS Paul Smith was in charge of the team at the cottage and the DCI had just given permission to go in. Paul was excited, he took it personally that Nick had fooled him, surely he should have known something was wrong with him. Were there clues he'd missed? The fact is that it is so difficult to tell, child sex offenders thrive by being invisible, Nick was clearly very good at masking his real personality. It is a truism that you cannot judge by appearances.

Paul's team of five house entry officers, dressed in all-black combat gear, surrounded the cottage quietly, covering every exit. The entry team moved to the front door with the battering ram, known to the police as "the large key".

Paul whispered knock, knock and nodded. The "key" was swung at the door which immediately opened with a crash, coming away at the hinges and falling into the hallway. The team rushed into the cottage clearing every room as they swept through the cottage, shouting incoherently, loudly and aggressively. The search team found a man and a young girl sleeping in adjacent bedrooms. The man looked shocked and the girl looked terrified.

Paul walked into the cottage and immediately realised that they'd got it wrong. They didn't look anything like Nick Webb or Kelly-Ann Miles. As Paul started to apologise, the man found his voice and started to shout at Paul and the officers standing guard in his room. The young girl was, very understandably, sobbing uncontrollably.

The man let out some expletives, then said, "What the hell do you think you're doing?"

Paul took the flack then calmly tried to explain what they had been doing knocking his door down. Paul was relieved to discover that the doorbell didn't work so the father assumed that was why they had not heard the police at the door. The fact was they hadn't tried to ring the doorbell so as not to alert the occupants, but Paul was certain that this information would not be helpful at that time.

Paul explained that they had had a call about a distressed child being taken into the cottage. The father told him that they had only recently moved there, and his daughter had been upset that her mother hadn't yet managed to join them. Whoever had seen them must have misinterpreted his distressed daughter's behaviour. "You didn't need to smash the place up, you only had to call, and you'd know we're not the ones you're looking for!"

Paul apologised again and promised that a carpenter was on the way. He then got out as quickly as possible. Paul felt bad about the distress he'd caused but what else could he have done, it all looked so convincing? He phoned DI Taylor and gave her an update about the operation. He'd classified the information as "false with good intent", there was no doubt that the call had been genuine, and they had to follow the information, but it was simply wrong, so where to now?

Paul's phone rang. It was DI Taylor. "Paul, get your team over to the address I've just texted you. The analyst, Sally, came up with a stroke of genius. She found Nick's original police application form, on it he had to put his parents' address. In his case there were two addresses as they must have separated. His mother had a cottage not far from Leeston, Peach Cottage, which was in a quiet and remote location."

"Had?"

"She died recently, according to the coroner's system we think her only son inherited the cottage."

"Nick?"

"Yes!"

"I'm on the way, let's hope we have better luck this time, that Sally's brilliant, remind me to buy her some flowers."

"I think she'd like that." Sue smiled to herself then hung up.

Chapter 37

It was early evening and a perfect time to be driving around the Forest. Simon Shaw loved the area and would often stop and walk enjoying the scenery, the colours and the wildlife. He started by driving around some more remote areas then headed towards Leeston to get a drink overlooking the Quay.

As he pulled up at the junction from Southway, Shaw got a glimpse of a grey Ford Focus driving by. Shaw was convinced that the driver was that detective, Nick Webb, although there was no sign of any children in the car. Should he call the police, but why should he do their job for them? On the other hand, Webb had clearly tried to stitch him up and revenge would feel good.

Shaw dialled 999 on his hands-free phone and after a few preliminaries got through to an operator. He pulled out to follow the car, making sure that he stayed well back, but wouldn't lose sight of the Focus. He told the operator that he had seen DC Webb who was on the news and was wanted for kidnapping that girl Kelly-Ann Miles. The operator seemed sceptical but took his details and said they'd be in touch.

Shaw was annoyed at the police incompetence but continued to follow the Focus at a distance. He was stubborn and wouldn't give up easily, after all if this was true then Webb had tried to get him imprisoned. When they stopped in a queue at a red traffic light, Shaw managed to note down the car's registration number. It was brand new, this was definitely not the car mentioned in the news, but wouldn't anyone change their car if they're on the run?

Shaw was unhappy with the response from the police and thought that he was just being brushed off. He decided to call DS Smith directly, Paul Smith had given him his work mobile number previously to keep in touch.

Webb was driving carefully, clearly not wanting to draw attention to himself. He was heading in the direction of Christchurch. Where were they headed? thought Shaw. He had to be careful to hang back, he had to make sure that he was not seen on the relatively quiet roads.

DS Smith answered his phone briskly, seeing that it was Shaw calling, expecting the call to be a complaint about his treatment. Shaw quickly explained what he had seen, and DS Smith got more interested. Webb was now on the A35 heading through Lindmouth and Shaw struggled to stay in touch in the heavier traffic. To his surprise, Smith seemed to believe him instantly. "OK, if you're sure it's him, stay with the car and I'll get some units towards you. I'll have to hang up to make arrangements, but I'll call you back."

Smith was relying on his own instinct, was Shaw telling the truth? He reasoned that they could have missed Nick, but to be sure he sent two officers to Peach Cottage while he diverted the rest towards Shaw's sighting. The sighting actually made sense to him because it was on a route from the cottage. It also seemed very likely that Webb would try to escape knowing he'd been found out. Webb had nothing to lose, which only made him more dangerous. Smith was taking a gamble trusting Shaw and the stakes were very high. He just hoped that Shaw was telling the truth.

Having quickly briefed the teams, Smith led a small convoy of three unmarked cars at high speed. The cars luckily had hidden blue lights which could be used in extreme emergencies such as this. The three cars moved quickly but safely, driven by trained pursuit drivers. Aided by the blue lights and sirens they made progress through the winding country roads to try to catch Nick Webb and save Kelly-Ann. Cars obligingly moved out of their way, but they were still a very long way away.

Smith then phoned Sue Taylor to give her an update. She agreed with Paul's assessment and promised to get a helicopter towards them as well.

Paul Smith contacted Shaw again and quickly got the update that he'd bypassed Lindmouth and was heading in the direction of Picton. Shaw didn't think he'd been spotted because Webb continued to drive slowly, with no sense that he was fleeing.

Shaw skirted Picton on the main route then turned onto quieter, country roads heading towards Ware. Both Shaw and Smith were having identical thoughts, what the hell was Webb doing, where was he going?

As Smith got into heavier traffic, cars seemed more reluctant to move out of their way. Paul, normally fairly placid, was furious that they were still struggling to catch up and felt a long way behind. He had notified Dorset police of what was going on, but there were no patrol cars in the area, just his luck! This should have been no surprise as Dorset is over 1500 square miles of mostly rural countryside, with only a small police force to cover the entire area. The chance of anyone being in the right place at the right time was slim indeed.

Webb seemed to be heading towards the Jurassic coast, but for what reason, what was there for him? As Webb came nearer to Wareham his driving changed, he started to speed up.

"I think he's spotted me," Shaw reported to Paul Smith. "He's driving faster now. I can keep up with him, though."

"If it gets dangerous, you have to stop," said DS Smith.

"Of course," said Shaw, with no intention of doing any such thing. Shaw was a confident driver but, more importantly, was bloody-minded and would not give up easily.

The Focus pulled away and the beautiful views, along winding country lanes, became more like green blurs. He stuck to minor roads, clearly hoping to shake Shaw off. Shaw's Audi was more powerful, but Webb managed to pull away. Ahead, Shaw saw the Focus pull out and overtake a black mini just before a blind bend. This was nearly calamitous as a large, powerful motorcycle came fast round the bend the other way. The Focus and the motorcycle missed each other by inches and Shaw could still see the fear and anger on the motorcyclist's face as they passed each other.

Undeterred, Shaw took his chance to overtake the mini and was rewarded with a single finger salute from the driver. Shaw had momentarily lost sight of the Focus but soon caught a glimpse of the rear brake lights ahead.

Shaw had no clue where he was as they raced through the countryside. He tried to give Smith any clue as to his location, only occasionally spotting village signs. As Shaw passed through the village of Steepe he was angry and frustrated to realise he had lost sight of the Focus. He couldn't believe that Webb had managed to get away from him.

He pulled over and thought, what if Webb had turned off, that would explain the loss? Shaw reported to DS Smith, who he heard curse, and then turned around in the next available turning point, which turned out to be a farm entrance a couple of miles along.

Shaw sat there for a while frustrated until DS Smith told him that the police helicopter had arrived in the vicinity. They had spotted what they think was the car heading down towards Kearsley Bay but had lost sight of it because of trees and were trying to find somewhere they could land.

So, he had turned off, thought Shaw. He pulled out onto the road, retracing his route and accelerated, picking up speed. After a few miles he spotted a right turn signposted towards Kearsley Bay. For some reason this meant something to him, and the turning was not long after he had lost the Focus. He turned right, hoping that the helicopter had seen the right car, and followed the road down to the bay.

He drove carefully as the road was single track shrouded by trees and high hedges. He didn't want to race past the Focus if it was parked up in a field. He wound his way down the road, then his heart leapt as he saw the car parked outside of the Purbeck marine wildlife reserve. The driver's door and the rear doors were open, evidence that the occupants had left the car in a hurry.

Shaw parked behind the Focus and updated the police. He got out and looked around. There was no sign of the fugitive in the visitor's centre and the staff hadn't seen him or Kelly-Ann. They suggested that people usually walk along the coast path, so Shaw went outside just in time to glimpse two figures reach the top of Hen cliff before they went out of sight again.

Shaw called out, but he was too far away and couldn't be heard. He ran towards the path which led towards the cliff top, then started to climb the hundred metre ascent. At one point, as it got steeper and became more difficult. Shaw thought why am I doing this? "Because I am not a bad person, in any case, he tried to frame me," he whispered to himself, but maybe it was time to prove it? Shaw had lived with his shame for so long that he felt the need to redeem himself.

When Shaw finally made the top, he joined the South West coast path. Looking east along the path he could see what looked like Nick Webb with a young girl. They were walking, seemingly in a hurry in the direction of Kearsley folly which was way too close to the cliff edge for Shaw to be happy. Shaw knew that the folly was a 19th-century tower built in the Tuscan style because he'd been there before, but it still looked anomalous, completely out of place on this Dorset cliff top.

He ran towards them with no real plan, amazingly they seemed not to have seen him up until now. However, as he got about twenty metres away the girl turned and pointed at him. Webb shouted at him to stop and Shaw did so.

"Stay away or we're going over the edge."

The girl clung to Webb and looked terrified. They were about ten metres away from the cliff edge, but Shaw could see the long, sheer drop to the stony beach and raging sea below. It was cloudy, gloomy and windy. A sense of impending tragedy filled Shaw.

Shaw called out "Look, just let the girl go and you can escape, I'll say nothing."

"It's too late, me and Crystal need to be together. If it means going over the edge, that will be your fault, you've left us with nowhere to go, we can't escape. Crystal, you agree, don't you?"

At this, the girl looked terrified, but said, "I want to be with you, Daddy!"

Shaw was confused, was this the kidnapped girl, he thought her name was Kelly-Ann, had he got this all wrong? "Aren't you Kelly-Ann? If you are, your mummy is worried about you."

"My mummy's dead, I'm with Daddy now."

Shaw immediately understood what was going on. Kelly-Ann had been groomed amazingly quickly and was now in thrall to this man. He carefully said, "Look your mum's OK, she wants you to be at home with her. Come over here with me."

"No!" shouted Webb. "He's lying, you must stay with me." As he said this, he started to pull Kelly-Ann towards the cliff edge.

As he said this the police helicopter passed overhead with a rush of noise. All three looked up but the helicopter just swept past. Shaw didn't know whether they'd been seen, but Webb had a look of indecision on his face.

Shaw tried to calculate whether he'd have time to grab Kelly-Ann if he rushed forward but decided it was too much of a risk, he'd never get there in time. He moved forward slowly and carefully, thinking quickly, where were the police when you needed them, what was that helicopter doing?

Shaw became aware of Webb looking past him towards the visitor's centre. Shaw turned and saw a small convoy of police vehicles arrive, where he had left his own car.

"Look, Webb, it's over, let the girl go, you don't really want to hurt her, do you?"

For the first time Webb looked really scared, he was sweating and looking around frantically, but there was nowhere to go. He could run, the coast path stretched for miles, but they would easily catch him, as there was nowhere to hide. Webb continued to move slowly towards the cliff top and was now only a few metres away from certain death.

The helicopter swept past again, it must have seen them, then banked left looking for somewhere to land.

Webb looked at Kelly-Ann and said, so that Shaw could also hear, "Crystal, there are bad people after me, the same people who hurt your mum, do you trust me?"

Shaw didn't hear a reply, but he saw Kelly-Ann nodding. Shaw moved closer as Webb reached the edge of the precipice, still holding onto Kelly-Ann who seemed frozen at his side. "For Christ's sake, man, let her go, it's not worth it, nothing can be worth this, please I'm begging you."

"Stay away from us, leave us alone!" screamed Webb in desperation.

Shaw glanced back and realised that the police were now halfway up the hill, heading towards them. The helicopter had landed in a field a few hundred metres away and several people jumped out so that they were moving towards the group in a pincer movement with the rest of the police coming from the opposite direction.

"Webb, you really don't want to hurt her, I know you care for her, let her come to me and give yourself up."

"I can't, my life is over, you've got me but I'm not alone. You don't understand, we need to end it now!"

Webb stepped towards the drop, pulling Kelly-Ann with him by the arm. Shaw lunged forwards, desperately trying to grab hold of something of the little girl. Unbelievably, Kelly-Ann squirmed free of Webb as he fell head first over the edge, and Shaw was able to get a good grab hold of her sleeve. As Webb tumbled over the cliff, Kelly-Ann and Shaw fell onto the ground in a sweaty heap, breathing hard and both shaking with fear. Shaw held her tight not wanting there to be any chance of her falling.

As the police finally arrived sweating and panting from their exertions, DS Smith looked severe and remarked, "I'm not sure you should be having unsupervised contact with children, Shaw."

Shaw was dumbstruck, he couldn't believe what he was hearing.

Smith continued, now smiling, seeing the look on Shaw's face, "Sorry, Shaw, that's an example of "cop humour", it's not always so funny to everyone. We saw what happened, well done, Simon, that was very brave of you. You saved this young lady's life. There was nothing else you could have done for Nick."

"He worked for you!" said Shaw.

"Yes, in that sense it's our fault, we missed Webb completely, and only found out about him by sheer luck."

Kelly-Ann appeared to be in complete shock, she said nothing and just stared ahead holding onto Shaw until a uniformed police officer, took her hand and led her away. "Come on, Kelly-Ann, your mum's looking forward to seeing you."

Looking at the hundred metre drop to the rocks and crashing waves below, Smith quickly concluded that no one could possibly survive the fall, in fact, even recovering the body would be a real challenge.

Epilogue

There was a slight delay before Kelly-Ann was reunited with her mother and brother. The police officer took Kelly-Ann to the sexual assault examination centre to be examined by a specialist medical examiner. To everyone's relief there were no obvious signs of sexual assault, but of course this was no guarantee that Webb hadn't abused her. Following the examination, she was spoken to by a child abuse investigator, but Kelly-Ann made it very clear that she did not want to talk about her time with Webb. Sue Taylor decide to give her a couple of days before trying again, maybe she'll change her mind when she's safe at home.

When she arrived at home she immediately saw her mum and brother waiting on the pavement outside her house. Seeing all the things she thought she'd never see again was overwhelming for Kelly-Ann. She ran over to her mum and brother, shrieking with joy and amazement. When her mum burst into tears, she and her brother joined in, all three hugging each other so fiercely that no one would have been able to separate them.

They were incoherent in their protestations of love for each other; even for her brother, Sam. Kelly-Ann tried to say sorry for what happened, but Julie wasn't having any of it. Through the sobs Kelly-Ann told her mum that she thought that she was dead, she'd believed what the man had told her. She had thought that she had no choice but to stay with him.

Julie told Kelly-Ann not to worry about anything she was safe back at home with her family again. Julie couldn't quite believe it. She hadn't given up hope but couldn't see any way that her daughter could come back to her. Now here she was, safe again.

Kelly-Ann was overjoyed that her mum was well, but she was still looking forward to seeing her room and Little Bear. When they went indoors she ran upstairs to be reunited with her favourite cuddly toy.

It took many years for her to come to terms with her experiences. She received counselling from a very lovely lady, but she would never give any real detail about what had happened to her. The only time Kelly-Ann made mention of Nick was when she told a teacher at school that her daddy had died in an accident, by falling into the sea. Over time, Kelly-Ann and her mother somehow found a way to cope, and things were good for the family, if never quite the same again.

Sam was overjoyed to see his sister again and didn't think anything of it when she occasionally referred to someone called Crystal. Julie, for her part, was just happy to get her daughter back alive. She was eternally grateful to Shaw for saving her daughter, but at the same time was very angry with the police about what had happened.

Shaw continued to work at Davies Engineering Industries and made himself invaluable. Shaw thrived on the challenge of his work and became firm friends with Jon Davies, the man who originally hired him. Shaw even managed to have proper contact with his son, Harry. His ex-wife flew back to England from America to visit her family, so all three met up for a sightseeing day in London. The day went very well, and Shaw had to admit that they both seemed very happy with their new life. At least Clay got on very well with his son, and they sounded like they were fond of each other. Simon couldn't help but feel a bit jealous of this, but he was glad for Harry. After this trip, the Skyping continued with considerably more success than the first effort. They'd found common ground they could chat easily about, and Simon enjoyed this.

Simon thought a lot about what had happened on the cliff. Had Webb released Kelly-Ann's arm so that he had been able to grab her? Had Webb, at the end, demonstrated some humanity to save Kelly-Ann's life? He'd probably never know, but it was comforting to think that maybe no one was beyond redemption.

His new lawyer, Debbie Martin, had turned out to be a good ally. It seemed that perhaps his original conviction wasn't entirely sound. During his trial, there was no evidence submitted that any of the child images had been viewed by Shaw, it looked like they had been downloaded in bulk with adult pornography images. There was clear evidence that Shaw had viewed many adult pictures but none containing children. He asked about the Thai DVDs but, apparently, there had been age assessments completed which had shown that the youngest woman had been twenty-one but made to appear younger. Again, this had not been disclosed by the police to his defence lawyer in his trial, so Debbie thought this was good grounds to appeal his conviction and maybe get it quashed.

Shaw regretted his first remarks to Debbie Martin, who turned out to be an effective and dogged advocate. With the help of the evidence which should have been disclosed to the defence in the original trial, she was building a strong case for appeal. But to what end? thought Shaw, his life had already changed forever. Still, it would be good to have a clean record and he would feel vindicated.

The coroner returned a verdict of suicide at Nick Webb's inquest even though the body was never found. DCI Jones, DI Taylor and DS Smith would always wonder what Nick Webb had done to Kelly-Ann and what had driven him, but they were never to find out. Several attempts were made to interview Kelly-Ann, but she would not speak about what had happened, saying that she could not remember. As is usual in the police, the detectives soon moved on to the next job without the luxury of dwelling on the last case.

Following a lengthy Independent Police Complaints Commission investigation, it was decided that no one could have foreseen Nick's actions, and no blame was to be apportioned. For Sue, this grated a bit because she thought that there should have been a better examination of why he was transferred to her unit, particularly when there were already concerns raised about his behaviour around children. Having been worried about his own position, Paul Smith was allowed to stay in offender management where his passion lay. As for Sue and Steve, they soon got an opportunity to work closely together again.

Simon Shaw maintained contact with the Miles family and became good friends with Julie, often seeing each other socially but with nothing more than friendship in mind. One day, they even went back to the same café where they had first met, but this time without the dramatic interruption by DS Smith.

Shaw would frequently watch the children who had both grown fond of him. One evening when Julie was out and after Sam had gone to bed, Shaw was watching a Disney film with Kelly-Ann on the sofa. She smiled at him, and he smiled back.

"Come and have a cuddle," he said.